THE GREAT KITTEN CAKE OFF

Anna Wilson lives in Bradford on Avon with her husband, two children, two cats, one dog and five chickens. She is the author of many young-fiction novels published by Macmillan Children's Books – and while many of them have been about pets, this is the first to feature cake-obsessed kittens.

THE GREAT KITTEN
CAKE OFF

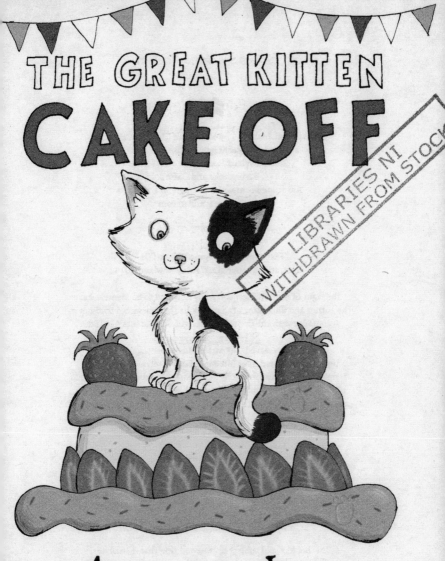

Anna Wilson

ILLUSTRATED BY ANDY ROWLAND

MACMILLAN CHILDREN'S BOOKS

First published 2014 by Macmillan Children's Books
a division of Macmillan Publishers Limited
20 New Wharf Road, London N1 9RR
Basingstoke and Oxford
Associated companies throughout the world
www.panmacmillan.com

ISBN 978-1-4472-7182-6

Text copyright © Anna Wilson 2014
Illustrations copyright © Andy Rowland 2014

The right of Anna Wilson and Andy Rowland to be identified as
the author and illustrator of this work has been asserted by them in
accordance with the Copyright, Designs and Patents Act 1988.

1 3 5 7 9 8 6 4 2

A CIP catalogue record for this book is available from
the British Library.

Printed and bound by CPI Group (UK) Ltd, Croydon CR0 4YY

For my family, who love cake and are great
fans of a certain TV baking show . . .
and for my cats, Ink and Jet,
who have been known to get their
paws on the icing at times!

I am really here. I have pinched myself hard quite a few times, so I know it is not a dream. Or a nightmare.

I have run my hand over the bright red work surface, touched the beautiful, shiny mixer and counted the different whisks and attachments that go with it. I have checked all the utensils and double-checked my ingredients. I have gazed at the colourful bunting which decorates the famous Tepee, and am now doing my best not to catch the eye of the other two contestants.

How did I get here, when only a few weeks

1

ago I had not been able to toast a slice of bread without burning it?

Oh no. There is one of the judges, Pete Jollyspoon. His fiery, ice-blue eyes look as though they could cut through steel, exactly as they do when he is on TV. There is nothing very jolly about him, that's for sure.

I take a deep breath to steady my nerves as the other judge, Milly Barry, gives me an encouraging smile. She is completely different from Pete, thank goodness. She looks less like a TV presenter and more like someone's lovely, friendly gran.

This is it, I tell myself. You *are* here, Ellie Haines. You have made it on to The Cake Off.

My mouth is dry. My heart is thumping. My legs are like jelly.

'Are you ready, bakers?'

'Don't let Pete put you off. He's always grumpy: the old silver-backed gorilla, we call him!'

It is Sam and Sid, just as chirpy, cheeky-chappy as they are when you see them on TV, looking relaxed and cheerful in jeans and T-shirts.

How *had* I got here? Certainly with no help from my bonkers family, who have always been hideously bad at cooking too.

No more time for nerves or questions. Sam Parkins is stepping forward to speak the immortal words that strike fear into every contestant's heart:

'Are you ready, bakers? . . . Are you steady, bakers? Then what are you waiting for? . . . BAKE!'

I had got myself into this crazy situation. I really had no one but myself to blame – me and my big mouth.

It began when I was hanging out with my best mate, Mads, after school one day.

'My life sucks!' I cried. I threw myself on to my beanbag.

'Drama queen,' Mads said, arching an eyebrow. 'It's not that bad, is it?'

'Have you *seen* my family lately?' I said. 'Charlie has always been the most irritating brother in the entire universe, as you know, but his latest obsession with trying to get on TV is driving me insane.'

'Oh come on, Ells,' Mads said. 'It's quite cute that he sends all those clips of his hamster into *SpringWatchLive*.'

'It is soooo utterly *not* cute,' I said. 'As if "Crisp Packet", or whatever his name is, is going to be the slightest bit interested in what Mumbles has for breakfast. He's not a wild hamster, is he? Anyway, that's not the point, I am sick of Charlie getting all the attention for his stupid plans.'

Basically, Charlie got all the attention in our family *whatever* he did. He only had to wear his pants on his head and do the 'Gangnam Style' routine to have Mum and Dad – and Mads if she was there – rolling in the aisles and crowing about how cute and funny he was.

Mads was still giggling. 'But he *is* so cute – and funny.' (See?) 'What about when he tried to get your Mum on *Looking Good Naked*?'

'Pur-leese! Don't!' I said. I held a hand out to stop Mads from going any further. 'I have just about managed to erase from my mind the image of Mum standing in her underwear asking Charlie whether she should go for "scoop-neck, V-neck or plunge-neck T-shirts" while he filmed the whole thing.' I clutched my throat. 'URGH!'

Mads was properly losing it now, rolling on the floor and howling with laughter. 'Your mum is so cool,' she squeaked.

'COOL? You are joking me! She is the absolute opposite of cool. She embarrasses me on an hourly – no, wait, *minute-ly* basis. I seriously think she is having some kind of Mid-Life Crisis. She comes out in public in her running gear to pick me up from stuff (and it shows off ALL her wobbly bits) and she *insists* on talking in what she thinks is some weird "down-with-the-kids" kind of language in front of my friends,' I said. 'She is *too old* to behave like this.'

'Ellie, stop it!' Mads said. 'You're being harsh. Your family are lovely. Look at the gorgeous birthday present they got you.'

Oh yes: the 'gorgeous birthday present', which was actually something Charlie had always wanted, not me. The 'gorgeous birthday present' which I was apparently now responsible for, especially when it caused havoc and mess which required *me* to clean up after it.

'The kitten, you mean?' I said.

'Kitkat, yes,' said Mads. 'What a lovely idea of Charlie's. I wish I was allowed a pet,' she added with a sigh.

I am not going to lie: Mads's mum is borderline OCD. There is a complete ban on pets in their house. There is a complete ban on a lot of things actually, which is why Mads practically lives round at ours.

At least her mum dresses like a mum, acts like a mum and talks like a mum. Unlike mine.

'Yeah, well, as far as the kitten goes, I would say "Be my guest", but I suppose your mum would freak if you took Kitkat home,' I said.

'You bet.' Mads nodded vigorously. 'Where is he today, by the way? I haven't given him a snuggle yet.'

As if on cue, there was a loud, protesting 'Raoooow' from Charlie's room, followed by my brother screaming my name.

'ELLLIEEEEE! GET KITKAT OUT OF HERE!'

'Not again,' I groaned. I pushed myself up out of the beanbag and made my way to my brother's room with Mads following close behind.

Charlie was standing in the middle of his bedroom, crying. 'He's got Mumbles,' he blubbed.

'Oh, my goodness.' Mads leaped into action and grabbed Kitkat, who was, sure enough, in the hamster's cage, an evil glint in his eye as he held the tiny rodent down with one white paw.

Mumbles gave a squeak of relief and rushed to the safety of his wheel.

'Charlie,' I said slowly. 'You weren't filming them again, were you?'

My brother miraculously stopped crying and swiftly hid his hands behind his back. 'No,' he said.

'Oh yeah?' I narrowed my eyes: I had already spotted his camera.

His face went red. 'OK, yes,' he admitted. 'But I didn't think Kitkat would try and actually

kill Mumbles. I only wanted a shot of him
stalking Mumbles. I was going to send it in to
SpringWatchLive—'

'Oh, for heaven's sake!' I cried. 'Just keep the cat
out of the hamster's cage and go and film some . . .
sparrows or something.'

Mads was tactfully backing out of the room with
the wriggling kitten in her arms. His black and white
tail was swishing and his right eye was flashing
dangerously from within its pirate-patch splodge.

'See what I have to put up with?' I said to Mads,
once we were back in the safety of my room. 'Dad
doesn't help either. He always tells me to be patient
and that Charlie's just "going through a phase", and
then makes one of his lame jokes.' I gritted my teeth.
'How come I am never allowed to "go through a
phase"? I think I'll have an Early-Teen Crisis – that'll
teach them!'

Mads was laughing again. 'This kitten is sooooo
wriggly!' Then she looked up and saw my face. 'Oh
boy. You *do* need cheering up. Come on,' she said,

putting Kitkat down. 'Let's go and watch some telly. It's *The Cake Off* in five minutes. That'll stop you frowning, Gloomilla.'

'All right,' I sighed. 'Let's bags the sofa before Charlie realizes it's on.'

I do love *The Cake Off*. Charlie does as well, unfortunately, which means I usually end up watching it with him giving me a running commentary on everything, trying to guess who is going to win and how long it will take before Pete Jollyspoon complains about another 'soggy bottom'. (That's usually when Dad comes in and makes jokes about 'rock hard buns' as well. Oh, how we laugh. *Not*.)

I think the reason Charlie and I love the programme *so* much is because our own parents are utterly useless at baking. Or any kind of cooking, come to that. Dad *thinks* he can cook. He is always telling us that his 'speciality' is cooked breakfasts. I'm not sure about 'speciality', but they are certainly 'special': burnt bacon, rubbery eggs, bouncy pancakes, and sausages that are so overdone you could use them as weapons of mass destruction – which is what it feels like they are doing to your insides if you try to eat them.

We tiptoed past Charlie's room, down the stairs and into the sitting room, with Kitkat padding softly after us.

'I'm serious, Mads. I can't carry on like this. I need a plan to spice up my life,' I said, while I fiddled with the TV remote.

'Like what?' said Mads. She plonked herself on the sofa.

'I don't know.' I shrugged. 'I just wish something *exciting* would happen to me. Life is so boring. School, homework, annoying little brother, irritating parents, pain-in-the-neck kitten— KITKAT! Get down from there!' I lunged at the kitten who was having one of his funny five minutes, leaping from tabletop to mantelpiece and now on to the TV, causing it to wobble dangerously.

'Come here,' Mads said. She patted the cushion next to her. 'It's already started.'

11

I grabbed Kitkat and sat down, holding him on my lap to stop him from escaping.

The presenters Sam and Sid were talking.

'. . . and if you are under sixteen and brilliant at baking why not enter one of the special regional Cake Off episodes which are helping to raise money for the very worthy charity, SportsFundUK? We're looking at applications right now. You can apply online. Just find your regional area on the map, click on it and follow the links.'

'Wow!' Mads breathed.

'Yes, so if you're a kid who likes to "use your loaf" in the kitchen,' said Sid, with a wink, 'why not give it a whirl?'

'A walnut whirl?' said Sam.

'Why not?' said Sid. 'Although we don't want any "nutters" on the show.'

'There's not "mushroom" for any more of those with you around,' said Sam.

'Oh, you are such a fun-gi,' said Sid. 'FUN GUY – fungi. Geddit?'

I groaned. 'Their jokes are even worse than Dad's!'

'Ellie,' said Mads. 'ELLIE!' She grabbed my arm and shook it. I looked at her and saw that her eyes were shining. 'Don't you think that's the answer to everything?'

'Eh?'

'This,' she said, pointing at the TV. 'It's the perfect plan for making your life more exciting. *And* mine!'

'Hisssssss!' Kitkat had started trying to escape.

'Ow!' I cried. 'Don't stick your claws into my legs!'

Kitkat hissed again and jumped on to Mads instead, where he rubbed his head against her hand and settled down calmly.

'Aww,' she cooed, stroking the kitten's fluffy white

back. 'Kitkat thinks it's a great plan too.'

'What are you on about?' I asked, feeling cross that 'my' kitten seemed to prefer my best mate to me.

Mads sighed. 'I knew you weren't listening,' she said. She nodded at the screen. 'This Junior *Cake Off* – I reckon we should enter. That really would "spice" up your life . . . geddit?'

I rolled my eyes. 'You're as bad as Sam Parkins – and Dad, come to that! You'll be "cracking bad yolks" next.'

'I'm *not* joking, though, I'm serious,' she replied. 'This is just what we need. Both of us! I'm going to do it, anyway. Oh, come on, Ells! Let's do it together. It'll be awesome.' She began bouncing up and down on the sofa. Kitkat didn't sink his claws into *her*, I noticed. 'Why don't we go and apply right now?' she said. 'Pretty please?' she added, pulling a face which made her look like more of a cute kitten than the real one sitting on her lap.

The trouble with Mads is, her enthusiasm is as

infectious as chickenpox: all it took was that glint in her eye, and I was hooked. Every time.

'Yes!' I agreed.

One tiny word. One split-second decision. If only I had known what I had let myself in for. 🐈

It's ironic, I know, but Mads is literally the only non-mad thing in my life. Although she can also be kind of crazy – but in a good, fun way.

Trust me, I have a million examples I could share with you. Like the time she suggested we swap clothes and pretend to be each other, to fool Charlie when he was little. It didn't work, mainly because we look nothing like each other: Mads has long dark hair and I have a short, blonde crop; Mads is feminine and petite and all arms and legs, and I am quite tall for my age and, shall we say, of bigger build. I have been known to be referred to as 'laddie' by visually impaired old ladies. No one would ever say that to Mads. So you could say that I was a tad *squished* when I wore Mads's clothes, whereas she positively *floated* inside mine. Which basically meant even six-year-old Charlie was not fooled by our identity-swap one little bit. All in all, not the most intelligent of plans. But fun. Good, crazy fun.

That's the thing with Mads: she will always come up with a bonkers idea which will cheer me up when I need cheering most (and possibly, in some cases, make me snort so hard with laughter that stuff comes out of my nose).

'This is the craziest of all your crazy plans, Mads,' I said as we made our way upstairs to the study. 'We should think about this properly, though. I'm not sure I'm the best candidate for *The Cake Off*, even if it is for kids.'

'Miiaooooow!'

'Cute – Kitkat's coming to help us,' Mads said, ignoring me. She scrunched her face up into the dopey expression that all people seem to use when they think about kittens. (All people except me, that is.) She bent down to talk to Kitkat. 'You think this is a great plan, don't you kitty-cat?'

'Raaoow?'

'Let's keep him out of here,' I said, glancing around the study. 'There's too much stuff he could ruin.'

'Awwwww!' said Mads. She dropped to her knees and began scratching under the kitten's chin. 'Little puss-puss,' she cooed. 'You wouldn't be so naughty, would you?'

'Mads, I'm telling you. He is a psycho cat. He has this insane split personality: one minute he's purry and gorgeous, the next his eyes have gone all I'm-going-to-put-an-evil-spell-on-you, and he's shredding my best T-shirt. He has scratched my bedroom door to bits and just last week I caught him with one of my old dolls doing something *unspeakable* to its hair.' I shuddered at the memory. 'I don't think we should let him in here. He might chew my parents' important work stuff or something.'

'It's fine. I'll keep an eye on him,' said Mads

distractedly. She had already logged on to *The Cake Off* website and was clicking her way through to the link for the application form for our region.

I gave up trying to talk to her and pulled up a chair. Then I eyeballed Kitkat. 'Just make sure you behave,' I muttered.

'Meeooow?' said Kitkat. He was sitting on a stool behind us, his head on one side and his glass-blue eyes wide and innocent in his most appealing pose.

It's all an act, I promise you.

I turned my back on him and focused on the web page Mads was poring over.

THE CHARITY JUNIOR CAKE OFF

The Cake Off team are filming a series of special one-off episodes of a junior version of the show. As well as encouraging kids to have a go at baking (and maybe give the adult contestants a run for their money!) the show will be raising funds for the well-known and well-deserving charity, SportsFundUK.

Do you love baking? Are you potty about pies and pastry? Bonkers about bread? Get in touch right now! World-famous bakers Milly Barry and Pete Jollyspoon are waiting to judge your skills and potential.

You need to be aged between 11 and 16 years old . . .

Mads had already begun typing in our names and addresses.

'Hang on a minute, I don't know about this, Mads,' I said. '"Love baking"? *Not* really. "Potty about pies"? Only if I'm eating someone else's . . .'

'Oh, please! It'll be wild. I *love* baking—'

'Yeah, but I don't. I can barely make cereal!'

'We'll do it together. I'll teach you,' Mads pleaded. 'It's just a "one-off episode" after all. They won't make us do all the things the adults have to do in the main show. And it's for "charidy",' she added in a silly voice. 'How can you resist?'

She was still typing frantically as she spoke. She has always been better at multi-tasking than me.

'Plus you said you wanted to spice up your life,' she went on. 'And anyway, you are dead artistic; there's loads you can do that I can't. I can bake, yeah, but I can't do all that fancy decorating business you have to do on *The Cake Off.* Together we will be the Dream Team: me the cook, you the arty one!'

To be fair, art is one of my few talents.

I grinned. 'Okaaaay . . .'

'You'll be amazing at all the creative stuff,' Mads continued. She was still typing. Boy, could she type fast. 'I reckon you could make the best Show Piece cake ever.'

I could feel the cogs in my brain whirring already as I thought about the Show Pieces I had seen on the programme. I would love to get my hands on one of those gingerbread houses. It would be so much fun designing the decorations . . .

'Thing is, Mads, it's the BAKING that is kind of important in all this,' I pointed out. 'When have I *ever* baked anything *edible* in the whole time we have known each other?'

Mads stopped typing, thought for a moment, then said, 'Cookies in Year 2.'

'From a packet. Under the close supervision of Miss Bates! And even then they tasted rank.'

'That's cos you had Play-Doh under your fingernails.' Mads chuckled. 'You *hated* washing your hands back then, so you just lied and told Miss Bates you had. The cookies ended up with tiny bits of blue and green in them!'

'Miss Bates said what a lovely idea it was to add chopped-up Smarties – and then she tasted them!' I guffawed.

'She nearly threw up – she looked as though she had been poisoned!' Mads added with a squeak.

We descended into one of our epic giggling marathons, the application form forgotten for a moment. Just then there was a loud hissing and yowling coming from under the desk.

'What's he done now?' I jumped off the

chair and dropped to my knees.

Kitkat had somehow got himself tangled up in the wires connecting the computer to the WiFi and printer. Dad was always nagging Mum to do something about the mess under the desk. I could see why now. It was insanely dusty and the wires were all knotted and confused – even more so now that my kitten was tied up in them.

'Oh, you idiot,' I said. I stretched my hand out towards Kitkat, but his eyes grew wide with panic as he struggled and got more and more tangled.

'What's going on?' Mads asked from above me. I could hear she had gone back to typing.

'Can you give me a hand?' I asked. 'Kitkat is stuck in all the wires. I'm going to have to unplug something.'

'OK, just a minute,' Mads replied. She was typing at lightning speed now.

'Mads, Kitkat is getting pretty stressed and it's not that nice down here.' I coughed. 'I'm getting dust up my nose.'

23

'OK . . .' More typing.

'Mads!' I shouted.

Just then the phone rang.

The sound made me start and I banged my head on the underside of the desk.

'Ow!' I crawled out, rubbing my head, and went to pick up the phone, gesturing at Mads to sort Kitkat out.

She nodded vaguely and carried on typing.

I picked up the phone with an exasperated 'Hello?'

'It's me.'

Mum. She always says, 'It's me.' Luckily I do not know anyone else who answers the phone in this way, or else it could be *very* confusing.

'Hi,' I said, still rubbing my head.

'Are you all right? You sound a bit off.'

'Yeah, fine. What do you want?'

'Charming!' said Mum. 'I'm calling to say I'm going for a run straight from work. I'll be back in time to make supper. OK?'

I was shaking Mads by the shoulder and mouthing: *Get Kitkat*!

Mads frowned and mouthed: *What*?

I rolled my eyes.

'Did you get that?' Mum asked.

'Yeah. I think so,' I said.

'Are you up to something, young lady?' Mum asked.

'Miiaooow!' cried Kitkat, emerging triumphantly from under the desk. He was trailing ribbons of thick dust behind him, but free from the cables, at least.

'What was that?' Mum asked in alarm.

'Nothing . . .' I said, nudging him towards the door with my toe.

'I can hear typing. Are you on the computer?' Mum asked. 'You'd better not be in the study with that kitten. The last time he went in there he got his paws tangled in the cables under the desk and got panicky and peed all over them. What are you doing in the study anyway?'

Peed on them? No! I sniffed the air experimentally.

25

'It's just Mads. She wanted to look at *The Cake Off* application forms,' I said.

'Cake Off?' Mum said. She snorted. 'Rather Mads than you! Can't see *you* turning your hand to baking anything, missy.'

Why was Mum *never* supportive of anything I wanted to do? She would happily cheer Charlie on for attempting to break the World Record for having the most snails on his face or entering Mumbles for *My Pet's Got Talent*, but when it came to me, well, everything was just a big joke.

'Have a nice run, Mum,' I growled. 'See you later.'

I firmly pressed the button on the phone to cut her off.

'Finished!' Mads announced.

The cursor was hovering above the 'send' button on the screen. 'So, are you ready, bakers?' said Mads, faking a Sam-and-Sid voice from the show. 'Are you steady, bakers?'

I thought about Mum laughing at the idea of me baking. I thought about how fed up I had been lately. I looked at Kitkat, who did look suspiciously as though he might have peed under the desk after all. Then I thought of Charlie and his stupid obsessions and Dad with his pathetic jokes.

Mads was right. This was just what I needed.

'The Dream Team?' I said. 'Why not?'

Mads grinned and clicked on 'send'.

A message immediately came back:

Thank you for applying for *The Charity Junior Cake Off*. Only successful applicants will be contacted by our production team. In the meantime, you had better get practising . . . So, what are you waiting for? BAKE 🐈

'So, did Mads enter *The Cake Off*?' Mum asked at tea.

'We both did,' I mumbled.

Charlie said, 'YOU? BAKE?' and made a big show of spluttering into his spaghetti Bolognese. (Mind you, that could have been because it tasted like slimy worms in a mud sauce. Yet another epic culinary fail from Mum.)

I ignored Mum and said, 'Shut up, Chazzer.'

Dad grinned and said, 'Sounds like a great idea. At last a chance to have your cake and eat it too!'

I groaned. 'Da-ad.'

'Unless you think Charlie's right and that it's a

28

half-baked idea!' Dad chortled.

I slammed down my fork and glared at my family. 'It was Mads's idea, and I reckon it'll be cool. Why is it that every time I come up with something you laugh and make pathetic jokes, but whenever Charlie thinks of some crazy plan you say it's cute and you give him loads of encouragement?'

'Maybe it's because I am interested in things I can actually *do*, like making films,' said Charlie primly.

'Oh yeah?' I said, turning on my little brother. 'Remind me what you were filming today? *Hamster Massacre*, wasn't it? Or was it *Revenge of the Killer Kitten*? Where is Kitkat now, by the way? Have you checked Mumbles's cage recently?'

Charlie went white and leaped from the table, pushing his chair away with a loud scraping noise.

Mum and Dad said nothing as Charlie ran from the room calling, 'Kitkat? KITKAT!'

'So how did you and Mads *cook* up this plan?' Dad began chuckling again.

'WHY can't you just take me seriously for once?' I shouted.

'Oh, Ells Bells,' said Dad, using the nickname he knows makes me cringe. 'Don't be so uptight. We're only teasing.'

'You are *seriously* winding me up now,' I said.

Mum gave another of her derisive snorts. 'You have to admit it is a tiny bit amusing to think of you creating anything anyone would actually want to eat. Let alone bake something good enough for that TV show,' she added.

'Oh, right. And what do you call this meal?' I asked, jabbing my finger at my plate. 'Spaghetti BOG-lognese?'

Mum gave me a dirty look.

'Just saying,' I said carelessly.

Dad grimaced. 'She's got a point, Kate.'

Mum got up from the table. 'Well, don't expect any help from me,' she said. Then she turned and added, '*Just saying.*'

This is always Mum's way of scoring points off

me – to copy the way I speak. Or the way she thinks I speak.

'Mads is going to teach me, actually,' I said. I got up from the table, leaving my tea barely touched, to make a point. 'She's a great cook and she thinks I'll be brilliant at the decorations you need to do to wow the judges.'

'That's true. You are very creative,' said Dad.

At last, a positive comment.

'I'm sure you'll be the icing on the cake!' he added.

'Please *stop*,' I said. I turned to Mum. 'So is it OK if we do the cooking here after school and at the weekends? You know what Mads's mum is like about making a mess in her kitchen.'

'Yes. I think you would describe her as "like, well stressy", isn't that right?' said Mum.

'D'OH!' I cried. 'You two drive me INSANE!'

The next day I arrived at school to find a bunch of Year 9s standing at the gate handing out fliers.

I looked around for Mads but there were so many

people crowding round it was like trying to find a needle in a haystack. (Except, who would seriously ever want to do that?)

I always feel pretty self-conscious around the Year 9s. They are only one year above us, but they seem so much more sophisticated. Especially Georgie Watson and her gang, with their perfect hair and shiny nails and super-tiny skirts. Not to mention their sharp-as-knives put-downs that always make me want to become invisible on the spot.

'Sign up today!' Georgie was shouting. 'Great practice for the real thing! And all proceeds go to the amazing charity, SportsFundUK . . .'

'Hey, Ellie!' Mads squealed in my ear. She had come up behind me. 'Today's the first day of the rest of your life, my friend,' she said, giving me a hug. 'We need to have a super-workshop-planning session later. I'm thinking, "Task: *Cake Off*".'

'Definitely! Let's get past this lot first, though,' I said. I took her elbow.

Mads shook my hand off her arm. I turned to ask her what was wrong and saw that she was staring at the Year 9s with a thoughtful expression. Georgie was still shouting something about 'signing up' and shoving fliers at anyone who walked past, but I couldn't hear what she was saying any more as there was too much noise from the people around us.

'Mads?' I tried to get her attention. 'Come on! Let's go.'

Mads wasn't listening, however; she was staring vacantly at Georgie. Or maybe it was not Georgie she was looking at, I realized, as I saw who was standing next to the older girl.

It was her twin brother, Ted.

Mads's face had gone a deep shade of pink and she started fussing with her hair and fluttering her eyelashes.

'Um. Mads, I don't think . . .'

Here we go again, I thought, as I watched my best

mate break away from me and sashay over to try to make eye contact with Ted.

Mads has been known to have some monumentally disastrous crushes in the past. I mean, don't get me wrong – Mads is super-pretty and lovely and bubbly and fun – but she always sets her sights on boys who could never possibly be interested in her. Everyone knows that it is totally uncool to flirt with anyone in the years above.

'Mads!' I tried again to get her attention.

Luckily Georgie stuffed a form in Mads's hands before she could get close to Ted and snapped, 'Move along, let other people through,' before fixing another charming smile to her face and starting up with her 'Roll up, roll up' routine.

'Ellie, look at this!' Mads yelled as she raced back and shoved the flier at me. She was practically squeaking with excitement. 'This is perfect! It's like it's *meant to be* . . .'

I ignored her babbling and grabbed her free hand, managing to pull her away from the crowd of Year 9s

34

while she waved desperately in Ted's direction. He finally saw her and smiled.

'Oh . . . my . . . gosh . . .' she breathed. 'Did you see that, Ells? Ted Watson just smiled *at me*!'

'Uh-huh,' I muttered. I yanked her into the main school building and made for the locker area.

'I can't believe it,' she swooned.

I opened my locker and began hurling books inside.

Mads had got sidetracked from our *Cake Off* plan already, I just knew it. One smile from a boy, and it was no longer *my* life she was interested in spicing up.

'Isn't this incredible? It's like the most amazing coincidence,' Mads was saying. She leaned back against her locker and gazed dreamily at the ceiling.

'What?' I said irritably.

'This,' she said, turning to me and flapping the piece of paper Georgie had given her.

I took a look at the brightly coloured leaflet. The letters screamed out at me:

IT'S THE GREAT OAKWOOD HIGH
CHARITY CAKE OFF!

'Oh, I get it,' I said. 'We enter this and you get to flirt with Ted Watson.'

'No,' Mads said. Her hot and bothered face betrayed her real thoughts, however. 'I was thinking of *you* actually. Well, *us* anyway . . . This Charity Cake Off will be fantastic practice for us.' She pointed at the rest of the wording. 'It's even raising money for the same charity as the TV show – SportsFundUK! It's a sign.' She sighed.

'Everyone in the school is going to be thinking the same thing,' I grumbled. 'We may as well give up now.'

'Oh, just read the leaflet,' said Mads impatiently.

FANCY YOURSELF AS THE NEXT MILLY BARRY
OR PETE JOLLYSPOON? YOU COULD BE
OAKWOOD HIGH'S 'TOP BAKER'!

BAKE A 'SHOW PIECE' CAKE, RAISE MONEY
FOR CHARITY AND HAVE FUN TOO.

ALL YOU NEED TO DO IS PAY £2 TO ENTER,
THEN . . . WHAT ARE YOU WAITING FOR? . . . BAKE!

'Seriously, Mads? Year 9? *Baking* in front of *Year 9*?
You really *are* bonkers. Do you have a death wish or
something? There is no WAY I am baking in front
of Year 9. In fact, why don't you
just do this without me? Imagine
Georgie and her crowd watching
me chuck flour all over myself or
whisk a load of eggs up my nose
or—'

'Will you just chill?' Mads interrupted. 'It's a cake
sale? You do the baking at home. There's nowhere to
cook in school, is there?'

'Oh, right,' I muttered.

Mads raised one eyebrow. 'So. All we need to do is
bake something and take it along.'

'You make it sound so simple.'

'It is. We can brainstorm some ideas for a really fab Show Piece. Come on, you know you want to, Mrs Artistic. Think of all the fun you can have with Writing Icing and piping bags. You could make the most creative cake anyone has ever seen. It'll be sure to catch the eye of the judges.' She leaned into me and gave me her most winning, Cheshire Cat smile.

Mads is so flipping persuasive once she gets a plan in her. She loves brainstorming, too. Brainstorming, workshopping, writing lists: she is the queen of organizational skills. She will go far.

'Think of it like this,' she went on. 'We can use it as a dry run for when we go on the real *Cake Off*.'

I shut my locker and looked nervously over my shoulder. 'Shh! Not so loud.'

Mads frowned. 'Why not?'

'Because I don't want anyone to know we've entered, that's why,' I hissed.

Mads tutted. 'I don't get you. You have been moaning about wanting to spice up your life, and then when an opportunity comes along, all you do is complain about it.' She looked hurt.

What if she *was* thinking about me in all this?

'OK, I'm sorry, Mads,' I said. I put a hand on her arm. 'I did think it was a really cool idea when we filled out the application form. I'm just getting a bit freaked now, that's all. I mean what if we really do get a place? Me and you on *The Cake Off*? With Milly Barry? On national TV? *And* –' it was time to voice what was really worrying me – 'what if they don't let us work as a team? I can't bake to save my life – as my family have been quick to point out.'

'Yeah, well, what do they know?' she said. 'You can do this, Ells. As for feeling freaked, don't worry! We applied together, didn't we? So we'll either both get in, or neither of us will.' She grinned and put her hands on my shoulders. 'If the worst happens and we have to compete against each other, we can still help each other out. I'd be just as happy if you won as if I did.'

'Me too,' I said, feeling relieved. 'Our friendship

is bigger than some silly baking competition. We are the Dream Team.'

'Too right. And imagine how infuriated Charlie would be if *you* got to go on TV!' she added with a grin.

'Yeah.' I grinned too. I looked again at the form for the Year 9 Cake Off. 'I am definitely going to need all the practice I can get, I guess,' I added reluctantly.

'So it's a yes then?' said Mads.

'Yes, it is,' I said. 'But only if you promise to help me and not use this as an excuse for flirting with Ted Watson.'

The bell rang for lessons.

'Pinky promise,' said Mads, offering me a little finger. Her eyes were wide and innocent-looking – rather how Kitkat looks when he knows he has done something wrong, in fact.

I should have taken *that* as a sign. A warning sign.

Mads persuaded me to go into town with her after school to get some ingredients from the cookery shop, Cakeland.

'OK,' I said. 'I doubt Mum has much in the way of cake ingredients. Um . . . Mads, are you sure you don't want to practise baking at *your* house?' I was starting to feel nervous about cooking at mine with my family there to get in the way and laugh at my efforts.

'You know we can't,' said Mads. 'I practically have to walk around the place on my hands these days to avoid bringing dirt inside.'

I laughed. 'You mum's not *that* bad!'

41

'You wouldn't say that if you had to live with her,' Mads replied. 'Hey, if you don't want to bake at yours, how about we go to your gran's? Grans are great bakers, everyone knows that.'

'What?' I spluttered. 'Sorry, but I was under the impression you had *met* my gran? I think you must be confusing her with someone who knows even the slightest thing about cooking.'

'Fair point,' said Mads. 'That prune-loaf thing she gave me two years ago is still giving me nightmares.'

I chuckled. 'And indigestion.'

'So I guess the *only* option is yours then?' said Mads.

I was not exactly thrilled at the idea. 'My family are already finding it hysterical that I am entering *The Cake Off*. I don't really want them around while I muck everything up. Charlie'll want to get involved. He's such a pain! Then there's Kitkat – we'll have to keep him out of the way.'

'Just chill!' said Mads. 'You worry too much.'

'OK,' I said reluctantly. 'I'll text Mum and tell her

we're going into town. I'll ask her later if you can come round and bake tomorrow.'

So that was how I found myself being dragged around Cakeland. Mads treats any kind of shopping like an extreme sport: count up the money, give yourself a goal, synchronize watches . . . SHOP!

I am not so keen.

'Just so you know, Mads,' I said, as we waited for the bus. 'I really don't want to end up spending a ton of money on this. I'm saving up for some new clothes.'

'Don't stress,' said Mads airily. 'Mum gave me some money when I told her we'd entered *The Junior Cake Off* and needed to practise.'

'Wow, that was nice of her,' I said. I couldn't see my mum handing over cash as easily as that.

'Not really. She went a bit green when I mentioned baking, so I kind of already promised we would be doing it at yours. She couldn't get the money out of her purse fast enough then,' Mads said.

43

'You are unbelievable.'

Mads grinned. 'That's me.'

We got off the bus and headed to Cakeland.

The window display was awesome: it was decked out in a summer holiday theme with sand to make a beach, and cookie cutters in the shape of shells and starfish strewn about. There were pastel-coloured buckets full of kitchen utensils in matching shades of pink, yellow, blue and green, and there was a huge gingerbread sandcastle in the middle, covered with sweets and icing. On top of the castle was a flag with the words 'Are you ready for *The Cake Off*?'

Above the castle, hung across the shop window, was a long line of pastel-coloured bunting with the words 'What Are You Waiting For? Bake!' written on the triangular pieces of fabric.

I felt my mouth go dry.

'Isn't it COOL?' Mads cried, gesturing to the display. 'I love this place!'

I swallowed. 'Mads, I – I'm not sure about this . . .'

Seeing the amazing window dressing had sent

waves of panic through me. I could not even face the school Cake Off, let alone the real thing. What had I been thinking?

'I think we should write to *The Cake Off* and say you want to do it on your own,' I said in a rush. 'I don't know one end of an egg whisk from the other.'

'Well, you must know *that*,' Mads said, frowning. 'Everyone knows that – the whisking end is the bit which is all . . . whisk-y,' she said helpfully.

I scowled at her. 'You know what I mean. I can't do this. I'm a terrible baker!'

I thought about all the episodes of *The Cake Off* that I had ever seen. The contestants had produced the most amazing creations. One guy had built a barn out of gingerbread with magical, delicate spun sugar all over it to make it look like it had a thatched roof. Another had baked a cake that looked like a swimming pool, with little figures made of marzipan swimming up and down in the bluey-green icing. I thought back to those Play-Doh cookies and winced. How would I ever be able to create a Show Piece, even with Mads to help me?

Mads put a reassuring hand on my arm. 'Don't worry, Ellie,' she said. 'This shop has all the right things for you to do the artistic bit. You are so clever, you'll be able to make something incredible. All you need is the right kind of decorations. We are the Dream Team, remember? You are not alone.'

I bit my lip and frowned.

'Look,' Mads went on, 'if you're worried about the baking bit—'

'The baking *bit*?' I interrupted. 'It's *all* about baking, you noodle!'

Mads shook her head. 'You'll be fine,' she insisted. 'You just need some practice. That's what the school Cake Off is all about. I'm sure you'll pick it up super-fast. Besides, you need to teach *me* how to do the arty stuff! Now, come on. We've got shopping to do.'

I sighed and followed her into the shop.

Mads became extremely excited at the sight of

the baking paraphernalia, picking up packets and shoving them in my face. 'Cookie cutters in the shape of poodles! Cupcake holders all the colours of the rainbow! Special squidgy icing thingummies to squidge icing on to cupcakes!'

I traipsed around after her as she picked up pot after can after packet of things I had not even known existed before that day.

'Look! We *have* to get these.' Mads was showing me some tiny silver balls. 'And look at this!' She shoved a can of edible silver spray into my hands.

We left the shop loaded down with silver bows, balls, sprinkles, cans of 'pearl powder' spray, tiny sugar butterflies, flowers, love hearts, roll-on fondant icing, food colouring, piping bags, icing sugar – you name it, we had bought it. And spent all the money Mads's mum had given her, too.

On the bus home I could not stop the nagging little voice of doubt in my mind from growing louder and louder.

'We've got a lot of stuff here,' I said, nodding at

the bulging shopping bags. 'Why do we need all this?'

'If we are going to stand out and get noticed in the school Cake Off, we have to do something *spectacular*,' said Mads dangerously.

'Cos this is all about getting noticed, isn't it?' I teased. 'By a certain Ted Watson?'

Mads immediately looked guilty. 'Nooooo!' she protested.

'So you don't think that entering this baking contest is going to get Ted to fall head-over-heels in love with you?' I asked with a grin.

'Of course not,' she said. 'I just . . . Oh, whatever. Here you are, take the bags. You will ask your mum if it's OK for tomorrow, won't you?'

'Sure,' I said, grabbing everything and standing up.

'We're *so* going to own this competition!' said Mads happily.

Personally, I wasn't so sure, but there was no arguing with her.

There was no getting out of the school Cake Off either.

We got back after school the next day to find Mum about to leave for a run. Again.

She has been doing this ever since she turned forty: she waits for me to come home and then dumps Charlie on me while she goes jogging around the park. When I complained about being used as a babysitter, Dad said I shouldn't worry, it was only a Mid-Life Crisis and it wouldn't last. Unfortunately Mum heard him and got cross. Dad tried to lighten the atmosphere with a badly timed joke about 'middle-age spread' (which sounded like a rather nasty alternative to Nutella), and that's when Mum started yelling. I put my headphones in to drown out the argument that followed and the words from the song 'We Are Never Ever Getting Back Together' filled my ears, which I thought was pretty ironic. Not that Mum and Dad will ever split up. He is the only one who can put up with her weirdness and she is the only one who can put up with his bad sense of humour. They are a marriage made in heaven.

'Hey, guys!' said Mum.

'Don't say "Hey",' I said. 'And what are you wearing? You're not going out like that, are you?'

'Cool jacket, Kate!' Mads gushed. 'Pink really suits you.'

'Thanks,' said Mum. 'Charlie told me that on *Looking Good Naked* they say that "black is very ageing", so I chucked out my old kit.'

'Pity he didn't tell you pink is very *headache-making*,' I muttered.

Mum frowned. 'What's that, Ellie?'

'Oh, she said pink is very *young* – er – making,' said Mads hastily. She hissed at me from the side of her mouth: 'Don't annoy her.'

I rolled my eyes.

'What's the matter, Ells?' Mum said, winking at Mads. 'Am I, *like*, embarrassing you?'

'Gosh, no,' I said with heavy sarcasm.

'Good. So, are you staying for tea, Mads? We're having toad-in-the-hole. Matt's cooking it when he gets in.'

'I wouldn't if I were you,' I said. 'It may contain real toad.'

'Oh, go on,' said Mum. 'It'll be SMF!'

'I – er, sorry?' said Mads, looking confused.

'SMF!' said Mum. 'It's text speak for "Super Marvellous Fun"!'

'It is *not* "text speak" for anything!' I groaned. 'SMF doesn't even exist. And no one in the twenty-first century says "super marvellous fun". Just stop it.'

Mum pouted and made a fake 'sorry' face. 'SCNR!' she said, making her eyes big and woeful. 'Which means "Sorry, Could Not Resist",' she added. Then she did the thing that is most guaranteed to make me want to scream: she clicked her fingers and waved her forefinger downward while waggling her hand and said, 'Get me and my street lingo.'

Mads was spluttering with laughter again.

I scowled and made do with a silent scream.

'Of course, soon it'll be Ellie cooking for the family,' Mum added. 'I hear you have a plan to domesticate my daughter, Mads? Good luck with that.'

I was fuming now. 'I thought you were going for a run?' I said, holding the door open for her. 'A *long* one,' I added.

Mum took the hint and jogged down the drive, her bottom wobbling like a giant pink blancmange.

I slammed the door behind her.

'Cheer up,' said Mads. 'You'll have the last laugh when you show your family what you can do in the kitchen. Come on, let's unpack the Cakeland stuff and get baking.'

Now that we were about to start cooking, I started feeling truly anxious.

'We – we didn't get any actual cake stuff yesterday, such as – I don't know . . . cupcake-y type ingredient-y stuff?' I said, playing for time.

'"Cupcake-y type ingredient-y stuff"?' Mads teased. 'You mean like sugar, flour, eggs and butter? Everyone has those things.'

'Maybe not my family,' I replied.

Mads put her hands on her hips. 'If your dad is making toad-in-the-hole there will definitely be flour and eggs,' she said.

She was patronizing me.

'OK, I knew that,' I said. I crossed my fingers behind my back. 'But what if we need, like, special sugar? Maybe we should leave it until Mum's done the supermarket shop.'

Mads tutted. 'You are such a defeatist. Mind you . . .' She began rummaging in a cupboard. 'There's a whole lot of rubbish in here.' She

53

started systematically emptying the shelves of jars and tins, most of which, knowing Mum, were out of date. 'There must be flour somewhere . . . Ah! Here we are,' she said, bringing out some more packets from the back of the cupboard. 'Self-raising flour and sugar. Eggs and butter will be in the fridge.'

She bustled over to take a look. 'Eggs – check. Butter – check. Great!' she said, all business-like. 'Right. Now, where's that cookbook your dad gave your mum?'

'*The Domestic Angel*, you mean?' I said.

Mum had gone bonkers when Dad had given her that. 'Domestic Angel?' she had shouted. 'I have no desire whatsoever to become a Domestic Angel. If you're not careful, you'll have an *Avenging* Angel on your hands!'

That had not been a good Christmas.

Mads had found the book on the shelves and was flicking through it. 'Cupcakes or muffins . . . there must be a recipe for those,' she was saying. 'You can make them look really funky, but they are quite easy to bake.'

'Good luck with finding anything "funky" in that book,' I said.

The Domestic Angel advertises itself as a solution 'for those who can't . . . or *won't* cook', which is probably why Mum tried to murder Dad with it. The recipes in it are rubbish: 'How to boil an egg', 'How to make a simple sauce', 'How to bake the perfect jacket potato', that kind of thing. I'm not surprised that Mum isn't interested in cooking if this is the only cookery book she has ever had.

'What've you got in the bags?' Charlie was standing in the doorway with Kitkat cradled in his arms and swaddled in a towel.

'Oh, go away and take that cat with you! It's unhygienic,' I said. 'Why's he in a towel anyway?'

'I gave him a bath in the basin so he's nice and clean. He had actually done a bit of a pee,' Charlie said. 'In your room, I think.'

'WHAT?'

'Yes, I think he's stressed at adapting to his new environment,' Charlie went on. 'Chris Packet from *SpringWatchLive* says that animals do that. I've filmed him doing it so that I can send the clip in for them to look at—'

'GO AWAY!' I yelled.

My shouting freaked Kitkat, who immediately struggled out of Charlie's grasp and made a running jump for the worktop, where he landed right in the middle of the tins and things. He sent a packet of spaghetti and a jar of tomato sauce flying; the spaghetti burst from the plastic and scattered everywhere, while the lid came off the jar, spurting sauce all over the floor. Kitkat made straight for the mess, dancing through it and redecorating the tiles with millions of tiny red pawprints.

'Great!' I exclaimed. 'You can clean that up, Chazzer and *then* you can go away.'

Charlie's face crumpled as though he was about to burst into tears.

'Oh, no, don't go away. We might need you,' said

Mads, rushing to put an arm around him.

'Cool,' said Charlie. He can recover remarkably quickly from being on the verge of tears, especially when Mads is there to give him a hug. 'So what is in those bags . . . Oohhhh!' Charlie shrieked. 'You've been to Cakeland. I LOVE that shop.'

'Freak,' I muttered.

'I do too,' said Mads. 'We're going to make some cupcakes with piped frosting and your clever sister is going to make them look totally amazing with all the cool stuff we bought.'

Charlie nodded seriously. 'Cupcakes are "This Season's Bakery Sensation", according to Milly Barry,' he said. 'I read it on her website.'

'"I read it on her website",' I said, mimicking my little brother. 'What are you, ninety or something? Since when did ten-year-old boys go on Milly Barry's website?'

'He's right, actually,' said Mads. She snapped shut *The Domestic Angel* and put it back on the shelves. 'That's a great idea, Charlie – let's look up one of

Milly Barry's recipes online . . .' She tailed off as she noticed my thunderous expression. 'Er, right . . . do you reckon your mum has cupcake cases anywhere?' she said, changing the subject hastily.

'She does,' said Charlie. 'In that bottom drawer with all the wrapping paper and silver foil and stuff.' He pointed at what Dad calls 'the messy drawer'.

I picked up a small bottle from the pile of Cakeland shopping. 'Peppermint essence. Bleurgh!' I pulled a face. 'What did you get this for, Mads?' I unscrewed the lid and sniffed. 'Smells gross.'

'Raaaow!' said Kitkat, padding up to join us.

'See, even the cat agrees,' I joked.

The kitten sat down abruptly and began to wash himself to get rid of the tomato sauce. He raised his back leg to lick it, and then toppled over in a backwards somersault. I sniggered.

'Peppermint cupcakes!' Mads said, her eyes lighting up. 'They would taste awesome. I bet no one else at school would think of that,' she went on, as she sifted through the chaos in the drawer.

'Especially if we add chocolate. Think of those chocolate-coated peppermint creams you can get. They are lush. And remember that mint cake stuff that we bought in the Lakes on the trip we went on last summer? You loved it. I bet that has peppermint essence in it.'

'Fair enough.' I had gone pretty crazy for that mint cake.

'Here's a peppermint cupcake recipe,' said Charlie. He had got hold of Mum's iPad (which she never lets *me* use) and was pointing at the screen. 'I found it on Milly Barry's website, actually.'

I found it on Milly Barry's website, actually: give me strength. 'Are you a member of her fan club, too?' I said.

Charlie stuck out his bottom lip thoughtfully. 'Does she have one?'

I rolled my eyes.

Mads had taken the iPad and was reading through the recipe. 'Yes, here you go, listen to this,' she said. 'Minty-Choc-Chip Cupcakes'.

59

For the cupcakes

- 225 grams self-raising flour
- 4 tbspns cocoa powder
- 1 tspn baking powder
- 225 grams caster sugar
- 225 grams unsalted butter
- 4 eggs
- 100 grams plain chocolate

For the icing

- 115 grams unsalted butter
- 225 grams icing sugar (sifted)
- 1 tspn peppermint essence
- food colouring (blue)
- 100 grams plain chocolate chips
  (or chocolate sprinkles)

'Oh right, so it's only the icing that's minty,' I said. 'Not the actual cake part? I guess that's OK.'

Charlie had picked up the tomato-splattered kitten and was talking to it in a stupid baby voice.

'Does Kittykatty think that Ellie likes the recipe?' he cooed.

'Shut up, Chazzer,' I said, throwing some kitchen roll at him. 'I thought you had some cleaning up to do?'

'Miiiaowww!' screeched Kitkat.

'Making the cupcakes should be the easy bit,' Mads was saying as she scanned the screen. 'All the work's in the decoration – and that's where you come in.' She looked up at me.

'This is so awesome,' Charlie cried, dropping Kitkat to the floor. 'I'm going to film you baking. If anything goes wrong I can send it in to *Barry Bill's Big Fat TV Bloopers*. You get paid £100 for every clip they show of people falling over or hurting themselves—'

'Chazzer,' I said. 'You are not filming anything. You are cleaning up this mess. And then you are going to *go away* and take *that* with you.' I pointed at Kitkat, who was now stalking a dry piece of spaghetti under the table.

'If you are going on *The Cake Off*, you will have to get used to being filmed,' said Charlie sulkily.

'He's got a point,' said Mads. 'Come on, Ellie, let him have a bit of fun. This recipe is so easy, I reckon we can't go wrong.'

'I hope this is not going to be a case of "famous last words",' I said with a sigh.

Half an hour later, the cakes were in the oven and the kitchen floor was relatively tomato-sauce free.

I was exhausted. I had learned how to weigh out the correct amounts of butter, sugar, eggs, flour and cocoa; I had spent a long time getting a sore arm beating everything together with a wooden spoon, and I was now pretty grumpy.

'They use mixers on the real *Cake Off*,' I pointed out.

'I love those things,' Charlie said wistfully. 'So shiny . . . I would have a red one if I could choose.'

'You really are weird,' I said. How many ten-year-old boys go dreamy thinking of mixers? I swung myself up on to the worktop and sat there, waiting for the cakes to cook.

'It's always better to do things by hand,' Mads said. She was still busying around the place, scraping the last of the broken spaghetti into the bin and wiping down the surfaces. Charlie had, unbelievably, offered to help her. (It's amazing the effect that girl has on my family. I think they would rather have her as a daughter/sister than me.)

Even Kitkat had not got in the way while we were cooking. He had fallen asleep in the now clean and tidy cupboard behind me.

Charlie was waving his camera in our faces again. 'How are we getting on, bakers?' he asked.

'*We* are not "getting on" at all, Chazz-Face,' I said, swiping at the camera. 'You and I will never "get on" at all if you keep filming me.'

'Don't call me "Chazz-Face",' he retorted. He blew a raspberry at me and ran out of the door. I was about to chase after him but luckily for Charlie, his life was saved by the sound of keys rattling in the front door and a voice shouting, 'I'm ba-ack!'

Mum came into the kitchen. Her jaw dropped as she noticed the cleaned, open cupboards and empty shelves. 'Wow. I thought you were baking, not spring cleaning,' she said.

'Yeah, sorry about that,' said Mads, blushing. 'We thought we'd sort through a few things. Once we started, we couldn't stop.'

Good job Mum hadn't come home earlier. An hour before it had looked more like a spring bomb-blast than a spring clean.

'Er, yeah,' I added. 'Some of those tins and things were well out of date.'

'You're probably right,' said Mum. Then her gaze shifted and she frowned. She was looking at something over my shoulder. 'OMG! Why has the cat changed colour?' she asked. She was pointing at Kitkat, who had somehow got from the cupboard to the window ledge and was blinking at us through

64

a face-mask of tomato sauce.

'Ooooh,' I groaned. 'Charlie was supposed to have cleaned him up. And don't say "OMG"! Why do you only ever do that when Mads is around?'

'FYI, he's your kitten, Ellie,' Mum said pointedly.

As if in answer, there was a retching noise from the sink.

Charlie chose that moment to reappear, and rushed over to remove a very sorry-for-himself Kitkat. 'Poor kitty. He's been sick,' he said. 'It must have been all that tomato sauce.'

Mum glared at me. 'I am going upstairs. Ellie – clean up that cat and get it out of my kitchen!' She had clearly dropped her I'm-such-a-cool-and-friendly-mum act.

'That is so unfair!' I shouted after her as she left the room.

Mads shot me a sympathetic look and said, 'Never mind, at least you've made your first batch of highly successful and delicious cupcakes.'

We looked through the glass door of the oven.

They did look good: perfectly risen and golden on top.

'See?' said Mads, as we got them out to cool. 'Ellie Haines: Top Baker. I have every faith in you. Charlie, you can help me mix the peppermint icing while Ellie cleans up Kitkat.'

'Great,' I muttered, grabbing my squirming kitten from Charlie and storming over to the sink.

Ten extremely irritating (and damp) minutes later, Kitkat was back in his towel, and I was scanning websites on the iPad for cupcake-decorating inspiration.

'Look at these,' I said, holding up the iPad. I had found some wicked blue and silver butterfly cakes which I was planning to copy.

Mads was totally right, of course: art *is* my strong point. Once I'm doing something creative, I forget any stressful or anxious thoughts I have and I just focus on what I am doing. Playing around with all the edible glitter and little sugar butterflies and stuff was exactly the kind of thing I love to do. It was like doing a sculpture, but with cakes instead of modelling clay.

I cut the tops off the un-iced cupcakes and then sliced those tops in two. Next, I took a blob of icing and put that on each flattened cake. The following step was to stick the two remaining pieces of cake into the icing so that they looked like butterfly wings. Then Mads and I painted the icing with streaks of blue food colouring and used the edible silver 'pearl' spray and an assortment of the things we had bought at Cakeland to cover the cakey wings in sparkly, glittery loveliness.

I wasn't sure that the cakes looked edible, but they did look beautiful. We had also managed to keep Kitkat out of the way the whole time by locking him in the utility room with a litter tray, to keep him from making a mess.

'Amazing!' said Mads, as we stepped back to

admire the results of our creativity. 'See – I knew you'd be great at this bit.'

'The ones you did look lovely too!' I said. Although, in my opinion, Mads's cupcakes looked a little more chaotic and wonky than mine.

Charlie sniffed disapprovingly. 'Definitely a case of "Style Over Substance", if you ask me,' he said.

'Yeah, well, we didn't,' I said.

'Pete Jollyspoon doesn't like "Style Over Substance",' said Charlie.

'Well it's a good job he doesn't go to our school then, isn't it?' I snapped.

'I think Sam Parkins would say that they look like an explosion in a glitter-ball factory,' Charlie went on.

I lunged at him, but he escaped and ran out of the kitchen sniggering.

Mads slung her arm around my shoulder. 'Don't listen to him. I think they look great,' she said. 'They've got va-va-voom.' She punched the air and laughed.

'I'm not sure cakes are supposed to have "va-va-voom".' I sighed. 'Let's just hope they don't give anyone indigestion, like Gran's prune loaf.'

'Oh, stop it – they're perfect!' Mads exclaimed. 'Our Dream Team cakes will steal the show.'

Even my family had to agree at tea that night. (Mind you, anything would have tasted good after Dad's toxic toad-in-the-hole.) We let everyone have one cake each and put the rest in a tin in a cupboard to keep them safe for the school contest.

'Amazing!' said Mum. 'I love the chocolate-and-mint combination. Very clever.'

'They taste like mint-choc-chip ice cream,' said Charlie.

Dad nodded. 'I have to admit, Ells, when you told us you were entering *The Cake Off* with Mads, I worried that it was a *half-baked* idea . . .'

'You've done that joke already,' I muttered.

'But now,' he went on, 'I might just have to *eat* my words.'

'Da-ad,' I whined. 'Please. Just. STOP!'

'He's right though, isn't he, Ellie?' said Mads. 'Together, we're unstoppable.'

I couldn't help smiling. 'I never thought I'd say this, Mads, but I am beginning to enjoy this baking thing.'

Me and my big mouth. Again.

The next day was a Saturday and Mads announced that we deserved a break from baking.

'The cakes are ready for the contest on Monday,' she said, 'and we can do more practice for the *real* Cake Off after school next week. I think we deserve a treat, actually – to celebrate the successful creation of our culinary sensation.'

'I'm always up for a celebration,' I said. 'What do you have in mind?'

'Well . . .' Mads looked shifty and then said, 'I have booked us both a spray tan in town today.'

'A *what*?' I cried. 'You are joking me?'

I hate spray tans! Not that I have ever had one,

but then why would I? Who actually pays money to look like a newly painted garden shed?

Mads shuffled awkwardly from foot to foot. 'I just thought, you know, it would be nice to look good for when we go on TV . . .'

'Mads,' I said. 'We don't even know if we've got through to *The Cake Off* yet. And anyway, don't you have to be over sixteen to get a spray tan?'

Mads raised her eyes to the ceiling. 'So? We *tell* them we are over sixteen.'

'There's no way that anyone is going to believe that *I* am sixteen!' I spluttered.

'OK, OK . . . You can have a manicure instead – how's that? I want to treat you. Come on!'

I have always wanted nice nails like Mads, and it was a very generous offer, especially as she had already paid for all the baking stuff. But there was something about this whole thing that didn't ring true.

'Are you sure you want a spray tan?' I asked. 'You've never even mentioned anything about tanning before. I just don't understand why—'

'Don't you *want* to look good for *The Cake Off*?' Mads huffed.

I hesitated.

'Well, *I'm* going. So – are you coming?' Mads turned to leave.

'Hang on a minute . . .' I said. 'When you say you want us to "look good for *The Cake Off*", you wouldn't be referring to the *school* competition, would you?'

Mads blushed furiously. 'No! Why?'

'I was just thinking that maybe you wanted to look your best for a certain Year 9 who will be judging it, that's all,' I said airily.

'Honestly! Mads cried, flouncing away. 'There's no need to go all MI5 on me. I just thought it would be nice.'

I hurried after her and put my hand on her arm. 'OK! Don't get stressy. Let's do it.'

Mads jabbered the whole way into town on the bus about how great the tan would make her look and how it would 'be totally awesome against my white jeans'.

'*Those* white jeans, you mean?' I said, glancing down at what Mads was wearing at that very moment.

'Yeah, why?' Mads asked, looking suddenly extremely anxious. 'Does my bum look big in them? I wore them cos I thought this outfit made me look older – you know, more like sixteen?'

Now it was my turn to roll my eyes. Mads practically doesn't have a bum, it is so tiny.

'Don't worry, the jeans are gorgeous. I'll back you up if they ask how old you are – and no, your bum could not look big even if you tried to inflate it with a bicycle pump,' I said.

'Rank!' Mads guffawed.

'So how much is the tan going to cost?' I asked, as we got off the bus. It had suddenly occurred to me that I'd heard these things were pretty expensive.

'Erm . . . twenty-five quid,' Mads said quickly.

'Ma-ads!' I protested. 'No wonder you have to

74

be sixteen! Who has twenty-five quid to waste on turning themselves the colour of chicken tikka?'

Mads broke into a run, which is always her way of dodging the issue as she knows I can't run as fast as she can. 'Here's the salon!' she shouted.

The minute we walked in I knew this was going to be a disaster. The place reeked of chemicals and the women at reception were the same colour as the desk. When they smiled, their teeth looked unnaturally white against their deeply tanned faces.

'Hi, you must be Madeline,' said one of the desk-coloured women.

'Yeah.' Mads avoided my eyes, which were wide with horror. She hasn't been called Madeline since we were at nursery. She *hates* her full name. Her family only use it when she is in deep trouble.

'Can my friend change her booking to a manicure while I have the tan done?' she said.

'Actually,' I said hastily, 'I think I might just sit and look at the magazines.' I had just noticed the woman's huge, fake talons with leopard-print tips. I

75

didn't fancy my nails ending up that way. For a start, how would I do any baking with nails like that?

'OK, babes,' the woman said to me. 'If you're sure?' Then she flashed a glow-in-the-dark smile at Mads and said, 'Just fill out this form. You are sixteen, right?'

Mads nodded vigorously, although the woman didn't seem to care.

'We'll be done in half an hour, right?' she said to me. 'Take your pick.' I flinched as she pointed an extra-long claw past my nose to where the magazines were.

You could have someone's eye out with those, I thought. I hoped she knew what she was doing with the tanning stuff.

I went to flick through the magazines and Mads followed the woman out to the back of the salon, saying something about Mads's jeans. Probably complimenting her on how ace they made her legs look.

So much for 'our' treat, I huffed. Still, it had been

generous of Mads to offer to pay. She knew how hard I had been saving up for some new clothes.

I checked out the perfect fan of reading matter on the low table.

A headline screamed up at me:

PETE JOLLYSPOON SCORES A BAKER'S DOZEN WITH MUMS!

Flip, I couldn't even get away from *The Cake Off* in a beauty salon. I picked up the magazine and saw that it was full of gossip about how 'mums' apparently found Pete Jollyspoon extremely attractive.

I shuddered. Can't say he does it for me, I thought, as I flicked through pictures of him posing with loaves of bread and looking moodily into the camera. If anything he's downright scary. Those eyes! Then I thought of Mum and realized *she* probably fancied Pete Jollyspoon.

I threw the magazine down with another shudder and found a different one about TV soaps. I soon got stuck into the gossip and forgot all about *The Cake Off*. I was deep into an article about how one on-screen couple were actually going out in real life when I heard footsteps from the back of the salon and a voice saying, 'It'll be fine, babes. It'll fade in a couple of hours . . .'

A dark figure followed her out of the back room. The person was vaguely familiar, but I was a bit distracted by the strange blotchy clothes she was wearing. I was wondering if it was some new kind of tie-dye fashion. (Since I am always the last to pick up on a new fashion idea, I am constantly amazed by what true fashionistas will turn up in next.)

I watched as the person paid at the till, then turned to me and hissed, 'Ells! Get me out of here! NOW!'

'Mads . . . ?' I was stunned. She looked . . . terrible! I gawped at her, not knowing what to say.

At last she gave me a shove towards the door and

we practically fell out on to the pavement.

'Don't say anything, please – I'll cry and it'll make everything worse!' she hissed. She was still pushing me along, desperate, I now realized, to get away from the salon as quickly as possible.

I had still not found my voice. My best mate was the colour of an antique chest of drawers, but, worse than that, I realized now that the blotchiness of her clothes was not an on-trend retro tie-dye look.

'Your lovely jeans!' I gasped, finally recovering the power of speech.

They were soaked with dark-brown fake tan.

'I don't understand,' I went on. 'I thought the tan was meant to go into your skin—'

'Not now, please!' Mads said in a shaky voice. She grabbed me by the hand and whisked me down a side alley and behind some large blue bins. As soon as we were hidden she burst into tears, which was unfortunate as it was making white-ish streak marks on her face.

'Give me your scarf,' she sobbed. 'I'm going to

have to get these jeans off before they're ruined.'

The jeans were clearly already ruined. I didn't really want my scarf ruined either, but my poor friend was not going to be able to walk to the bus wearing them as they were.

Mads was yanking at her jeans, struggling to get them off.

'You can't take your clothes off in the middle of town!' I cried.

'I don't have much choice!' Mads wailed. She grabbed my scarf and proceeded to wind it around her legs in an attempt to make it into a makeshift skirt. Luckily it was a sunny day and plenty of people were going around in short skirts. Plus, Mads would look good in a bin bag, and the scarf was wide and long, so it did look pretty convincing.

'We'll have to get a taxi back to your place,' she sobbed. 'Do you have any money? As you weren't getting your nails done I spent the extra on having the "de luxe" service. What a joke!'

'But . . .' I protested, thinking of the new clothes

I had *almost* enough money to buy.

'I'll get my dad to pay you back,' she pleaded.
'*Please!* I can't get the bus looking like this.'

So, as always, Mads got her way.

In the taxi I asked Mads if she wanted me to come back home with her and help her explain the state of her jeans to her mum, who was sure to freak when she saw them.

'Or I could provide a distraction while you nip in and stick them in the wash,' I offered. 'I'm sure if you use some of that white-out stuff they'll come up as good as new. If it can get grass stains out of Charlie's clothes when he's been lying in the mud filming fox dens, then it can get stains out of anything.'

Mads sniffed. 'No, it's OK,' she said. 'I just want to be on my own. I can handle Mum. See you on

Monday. I'll be in the shower until then, trying to scrub this lot off.'

She held out her streaky arms, and her face crumpled again.

'Oh, Mads, I'm so sorry,' I said. 'I'm sure you'll be OK by Monday.'

'I'd better be!' she said. She wiped her nose on her wrist. 'You just look after those cupcakes, all right? As long as they get to school in one piece looking fabulous, we will totally own that contest.'

I smiled. 'That's better,' I said. 'The old Mads is back!' I gave her a quick squeeze as the taxi pulled up outside her house. 'See you at school,' I said.

'Yeah, see ya.' Mads got out. 'I *will* pay you back,' she added.

I nodded and shut the car door.

Don't forget the cakes! she mouthed through the window.

As if I could forget anything to do with cakes for more than five minutes of my life, I thought.

'I'm home!' I shouted, as I pushed open the front door.

'About time, too,' said Mum, who was coming down the hall (in her running gear, of course) like a neon-pink bat out of hell.

'Hi,' I said. 'Whassup?'

'I'll tell you "whassup", madam,' she said. 'In fact, I will *show* you "whassup".' She grabbed my arm and pulled me into the kitchen. 'THIS,' she said with a dramatic sweep of her free hand, 'is "whassup".'

I was stunned for the second time that afternoon. The sight before me was a million times more alarming that Mads's freaky fake-bake. The kitchen looked as though someone had picked it up, turned it upside down and given it a good shake. The contents of the cupboards were all over the work surfaces: spilt food was smeared over the floor, walls and table, and there were boxes, sachets and tins everywhere. One tin in particular caught my eye. I tried very hard not to look at it. Maybe if I pretended I hadn't seen it, it wouldn't be real.

84

'I go out an hour for my morning run, and I come home to find the kitchen looking like a bomb has hit it! What were you thinking? I thought I asked you to tidy up after your baking?' Mum snarled. I was pretty sure actual steam was coming out of her ears and her face was dangerously red. Not a great accessory to the pink sports kit.

'I – I've been out,' I said. 'I haven't done any baking today.'

'Right,' said Mum. 'So I suppose the fairies did this?'

She pointed to the chaos.

'It . . . it could have been Charlie,' I said. I realized how lame I sounded, but seriously? Mum must have known I wouldn't leave the kitchen in this kind of state.

'Charlie has been at Gran's,' said Mum. 'He's still there. So, no, I don't think this could have been Charlie.' She scowled at me for a beat before throwing her hands in the air. 'Well, don't just stand there!' she cried. 'Get the broom and some cloths

85

and get cleaning. I will be in the shower.'

I waited until Mum had stomped upstairs, muttering under her breath, and then I walked very slowly to the tin which was worrying me the most.

It was the tin Mads had put the cupcakes in.

Please don't let them be ruined, I prayed helplessly. It was upside down, though, and the lid appeared to have come off.

This did not bode well.

I lifted the tin, feeling as though everything was happening in slow motion.

'NO!'

I sat there, staring at the mess before me. Our once beautiful Mint-Choc-Chip Butterfly Cupcakes stared back at me. They were certainly not beautiful any more. They were not even cupcakes any more. They were a congealed sludgy mess of smeared icing, squashed cake and destroyed decorations. Completely unsalvageable.

I was too shocked to even shed a tear. 'How on earth . . . ?' I said aloud. 'They were inside a tin, inside a *cupboard*, for heaven's sake . . .'

Then, as if in answer, there came a tiny
'Meeooow', from right inside the very cupboard
where the cake tin had been placed.

'No,' I said again. 'No-no-no-no-no-no-no, this is
NOT happening.'

'Miaaaaoooow!' said Kitkat again, louder this
time.

I tiptoed around the mess on the floor and made
my way towards the cupboard.

'Where are you?' I felt around inside, behind
the few packets and tins that were still there,
until I caught hold of something soft and furry.
And sticky.

'Eeuw!' I pulled my kitten out and held him up
by the scruff of the neck. 'Why?' I cried. 'What are
you trying to do to me?' He was covered in blue and
white icing and smelt pretty bad. Holding on to him
more firmly as he started to wriggle, I peered again
into the cupboard.

'You've been sick,' I said. 'That's just great. GREAT!

Well, I can't say I am surprised. What were you doing eating *cake*?'

'It was probably the butter in the icing,' said a voice behind me.

I whirled around, Kitkat swinging precariously in my hand.

'Chazzer . . .' I growled.

'It's not my fault,' said my little brother. He threw his hands up in defence. 'I wasn't even here. Dad's just brought me back from Gran's. You should have checked the cupboards were shut properly. Kitkat got in there before, didn't he . . . ?'

'OK, thanks for the advice,' I sneered. 'Bit late in the day now.'

'Raaow.' Kitkat had started lashing out with his claws and was struggling hard.

'Put him down,' said Charlie. 'He doesn't like being held like that.'

'And I don't like having my hard work destroyed!' I yelled. 'What is Mads going to say? She'll go crazy.'

Charlie took a step towards me and grabbed Kitkat.

I was going to have to start a whole new batch of cakes. On my own.

'Just get out,' I said to Charlie. 'And take that rank animal with you. I don't want him in the kitchen *ever* again. I don't care if he *murders* Mumbles. He can stay in your room from now on.'

'Yes, Mum,' Charlie said. He stuck his tongue out. I must have looked as though I meant business, however, because he backed out of the room and took Kitkat with him.

He had to have the last word, though.

'Actually, this is good experience,' he called out over his shoulder.

'Oh yeah? And how did you work that one out?' I said.

'You'll need to learn how to "Turn Disasters Into Triumphs" if you get on *The Cake Off*,' he said. 'That's what Milly Barry always says.'

Then he shot me a cheeky grin and disappeared up the stairs.

By the time I had finished cleaning up I had worked myself into a right state. I couldn't stop thinking about how Mads would react once I told her what had happened.

Even if I explained that it was actually Kitkat's fault, she would definitely flip. She was already so upset because of the fake-tan disaster. Now I had made things worse by mucking up our chances at the school Cake Off, which meant I had also probably trashed her chances with Ted.

There was only one thing for it. I needed to fix this mess, and I was going to have to do it on my own.

I grabbed Mum's iPad and flicked through page after page of Milly Barry's website in a panic, trying to find the right recipe.

'Come on,' I said to myself. 'You have got to make this right. If you can't do this, then there's no way you can succeed on the real *Cake Off*.'

At last I found the recipe.

I took a deep breath. 'First things first. Bake the cakes.'

I thought hard about everything Mads had told me about mixing together the butter and the sugar, and soon I was into the swing of it. I scooped the mixture into the cupcake cases, feeling very proud. It looked just like the mix I had made with Mads.

I checked the oven was at the right temperature, put the cakes in and sat back to relax with a glass of juice to watch them through the glass door.

Wow, they *are* rising fast, I thought, as I sipped my drink. I don't remember them doing that last time. I wonder if I should get them out and . . . OH!

One of the cakes suddenly exploded and fell in

on itself like a reverse volcano.

'*No!* NO!' I cried, leaping up from my chair and waving my hands as though the cakes could hear me.

I turned the oven off just as two more cupcakes exploded.

'What shall I do?' I hopped from one foot to the other.

POP! POP! POP! SPLAT!

The remaining cakes burst out of their cases and covered the glass door of the oven with a gloopy mess.

Charlie had come running at the sound of my screams.

'Ah . . . Too much baking soda,' he said, shaking his head sadly.

'WHAT?'

'It's half a *tea*spoon of soda. You must have used half a *table*spoon,' he pointed out, showing me the recipe.

I had, but there was no way I was going to admit this to my know-it-all brother.

'How on earth am I supposed to know that?' I said.

 92

Charlie gave a condescending smile. '"Tspn" means teaspoon and "tbspn" means tablespoon,' he said. 'Everyone knows that. You need to "GET A GRIP!" as Sam and Sid would say.'

'I'll get a grip on you if you're not careful – around YOUR NECK,' I shouted.

But Charlie was not taking the hint. 'I am getting my camera for this,' he said, beaming. 'It's better than "Doughgate".'

'What the flip is "Doughgate"?' I snarled.

'Don't you remember? It was a moment of TV gold! One of *The Cake Off* contestants stole another baker's dough and Sam and Sid said—'

'Chazzer. Shut. Up. Now. Before I do something we will both regret,' I warned.

Charlie made a *Woooooo*-sound and ran off, laughing.

'IDIOT,' I shouted after him.

I huffed and puffed as I got to work cleaning up, determined to make the cakes work the second time around.

93

Once the cupcakes were in the
oven I turned my attention to
finding the peppermint essence.
Mads and I had only used a small
quantity before, so there ought to
have been loads left over.

However, I couldn't find it anywhere.

Kitkat must have spilt it in his rampage around
the kitchen, I thought. Or maybe I chucked it in the
bin with the other stuff I threw away when I was
clearing up?

I was despairing now. I looked at the bin. There
was no way I was going to empty that and sort
through it.

'Maybe it doesn't matter if I don't make them
peppermint-flavoured,' I said to myself. 'Mads isn't
going to taste them, so she'll never know.'

Deep down, however, I knew this was not the
case: Mads would find out when she entered them
for the contest as 'Mint-Choc-Chip' cakes. The judges
would comment on the fact that they tasted just like

normal, boring cupcakes, and then I would have to admit what had happened and Mads would be even more furious with me.

'I shall just have to improvise,' I muttered.

'Talking to yourself, big sis?'

Charlie was back. With his flipping camera.

I was about to yell at him to GET OUT when I realized that, for once, I could put his ridiculous obsession with *The Cake Off* to good use.

'Seeing as you are such a genius know-it-all nerd,' I said, '*you* are going to have to think of a way to flavour these cakes with peppermint when there's no peppermint essence left.'

'Say please,' Charlie demanded, pointing the camera right into my face.

'*Please*, Charlie,' I said.

He gave me a smug grin and said, 'I'll get my thinking cap on!'

Why I ever thought I could rely on my brother to give me advice, I do not know.

I would certainly live to regret it. 🐈

Luckily Mads was in a great mood after the weekend. She had had the whole of Sunday to hide away from the world and shower for England, which meant that by Monday morning her streaky creosote fake-bake had faded, but secretly I thought she still looked as though she had fallen into a swimming pool full of brown sauce. Not that I would have dared say so. In any case, I was a bundle of nerves about the replacement cakes.

'Oh good, you remembered them,' she said, noticing the tin. (I had been careful to put them in the same one we had used before.)

'I could hardly forget with you texting me every

five minutes yesterday,' I pointed out. 'I don't know why you didn't come round and watch me pick them up this morning.'

'Yeah, well, I needed a last minute shower-and-exfoliate session, just to be on the safe side,' she said. She checked the skin tone of her arms for the millionth time that morning. 'It looks great now, doesn't it?' she asked.

I recognized a tiny note of anxiety in her voice, so I beamed and said, 'You look gorgeous.' What are best mates for?

'Thanks, Ells. And if anyone says anything, I'll just tell them I went on a mini-break over the weekend.'

'Yeah.' It was all I could trust myself to say. The more I looked at her, the more I noticed that her eyes and teeth were so white against the tone of her skin that they looked radioactive. No one would believe it was a natural tan.

I have to admit, I was selfishly rather relieved that Mads was so preoccupied with her looks. It meant that she hadn't once thought to check the cakes: I had spent all weekend worrying that she would. I was convinced she would be able to tell right away that they weren't the originals.

As soon as we got to school I put the cakes in my locker and made myself forget about them.

By the afternoon I was actually feeling quite calm.

Mads, in total contrast, was a jittery bag of nerves. She kept rushing into the cloakrooms to check her make-up and fuss with her hair every chance she got.

'You are *so* not interested in the cake part of this contest, are you, Mads?' I teased, hoping this was true.

'What?' Mads asked. She put on her most innocent expression.

'Well, put it this way: it's not our baking you're hoping to impress the judges with, is it?' I said. 'Or rather, one judge in particular . . .'

'Shut up,' said Mads. She didn't deny it, though.

The minute the bell went for the end of the day, Mads was off at top speed in the direction of the school hall. She reminded me of Kitkat skittering around the place when he has one of his funny five minutes.

My journey to the hall, on the other hand, was tortuous. I was carrying the cakes and had to try to avoid being jostled while crowds of pupils headed for the school exit. They streamed out at top speed, like caged animals released into the wild.

I wished I could join them.

When I finally arrived in the hall, Mads had already disappeared into the throng. I stopped in the doorway and scanned the room.

There was a huge banner slung across the top of the stage which read: 'Welcome to the Oakwood High Charity Cake Off'. It was decorated with silver stars and glitter.

'See? Our cakes tie in with the theme,' said a giddy voice behind me.

'Flip! Where did you spring from?' I said, as the cakes rattled in the tin. 'You scared the life out of me, Mads – I nearly dropped everything.'

'Never mind that.' Mads leaned in. 'Have you seen him?' She nudged me, knocking the cake tin, and nodded towards the stage.

A couple of people parted at that moment to reveal the person Mads was talking about.

Ted Watson. Officially the hottest guy in Year 9. If you are into that kind of thing. Which I most definitely was not.

'Oh. Oh. I am going to die. Right here. On. The. Spot,' said Mads.

The object of Mads's death wish was completely unaware of the commotion he was causing. He was engrossed in setting up the baking-display tables with a bunch of his mates and his twin sister Georgie.

'I am dying, it is official,' cried Mads. She was flapping her hands in front her face, the way people do on telly when they are trying not to get over-emotional.

Yeah, and anyone who eats these cakes will probably die too, I thought to myself. My nerves were getting the better of me again, fluttering around my stomach like the butterfly decorations on the stupid cupcakes. I was beginning to think that, not only did they not look as great as the originals had done, they were probably not going to taste that marvellous either, what with Charlie's 'genius' idea at improvising the peppermint flavouring.

'Don't die, Mads,' I joked, to cover my own nerves. 'It's against Health and Safety to die when there's food around.'

'Shhh! You're embarrassing me,' Mads said in a low voice. Then she caught Ted's eye – and he only went and smiled. 'Oh, he's soooo fit,' she said in a gooey whisper. 'You see he's had his hair cut? It makes him look just like Larry Files from Wrong Direction! And his eyes – I swear they're extra blue today,' she swooned.

'Great. They'll match the icing on our cupcakes then,' I quipped.

Inwardly, I was cursing Ted's new

Larry Files looky-likey haircut. It would mean Mads would fall even more hopelessly head-over-heels than she already had. Mads ADORES Larry Files. Her bedroom is literally plastered with his face and stupid floppy hair and she plays Wrong Direction's greatest hits on a loop until I feel ready to commit grievous bodily harm on her iPod.

I sighed. I was going to have to tread carefully here.

'Mads,' I said. 'Do you really think Ted's going to notice – I mean, I don't mean to be rude, but, don't you worry that he might be a bit . . . out of your league? No, um, what I mean is . . . he's in Year 9 . . .' I tailed off. Wow, that went well, I thought.

Mads had stopped in her tracks. Her face was thunderous. '*Out of my league?*' she spat. 'Why don't you tell me *exactly* what you "mean", Ellie?'

'No, what I meant was: Oh no! We really are going to be judged by the Year 9s. That's way out of *our* league . . .' I was *so* not handling this well. 'I mean, I thought it would be the teachers judging it.'

I bit my lip and decided to shut up.

Mads scrutinized me before saying, 'You know what they say about being in a hole? If you dig any deeper, you'll fall right in and they'll have to send out a search party.'

Not a bad idea, in the circumstances, I thought.

Then Ted smiled at us again and Mads seemed to forget I had insulted her. She flashed him an insane grin back.

'Just remember, Ells,' she muttered through her smile. 'We're here to win: eyes on the prize!'

'OK,' I muttered. I think I know what prize *you're* talking about, I thought.

Then she grabbed the tin from me and with a purposeful flick of hair she announced, 'Our cakes are glitzy and sparkly and glam. We *will* wow the judges.'

'Isn't the proof of the pudding in the eating?' I pointed out. 'That's what Milly Barry says on *The Cake Off*, anyway.'

I might as well have been talking to myself. Mads

was already strutting her stuff towards Ted and the other Year 9s.

I felt smaller and smaller with every step she took away from me. How come she had so much confidence, even in a situation like this? I observed how she pushed through the Year 9s to get the best spot for our cakes. She didn't seem to notice people looking her up and down and giggling at her tan. She could have been wearing a comedy wig and glasses and she would still have been able to carry it off as though it was the most normal thing in the world.

She started talking to Ted, then looked over at me, raising her eyebrows in a code I knew all too well. In other words: 'He's *soooo* gorgeous!'

The second she did that, something that had been niggling at the back of my mind leaped into focus. What if Mads had an ulterior motive for entering *The Cake Off* TV show? She had been pretty quick off the mark getting our applications in. The more I watched her with Ted, and the more I thought about it, the more I began to suspect she was up to something. What if this whole plan of hers – the school Cake Off, applying for the TV show, the outing to the salon – had nothing to do with spicing up *my* life, and everything to do with spicing up hers?

Mads was in full-on flirt mode now, flicking her hair, striking a pose, laughing at what Ted was saying. I might as well have been invisible, now that she had his full attention.

I became more and more suspicious. Were her feelings linked with her sudden urge to excel at baking? Was it possible that she knew something I didn't? Like, for instance, had Ted entered the TV contest as well? It was a possibility that the *only* reason Mads had wanted us to apply for *The Cake Off* TV show in the first place was because she had found out that Ted was planning to enter too. Especially as she knew I couldn't bake for toffee. Maybe her real plans had nothing to do with the Dream Team . . .

Maybe she had her sights set on joining Team Ted instead.

I felt an overwhelming desire to turn around and walk out, leaving Mads to her scheming.

But something held me back. Mads was my best mate, after all. We had been best friends since nursery school. Maybe, just maybe, I was wrong. Maybe it was only my nerves about the replacement cakes getting the better of me.

I decided to give Mads the benefit of the doubt. I pulled myself together and made my way steadily towards her.

'I think the cakes will look great right here,' she was saying, giving them a shove into the centre of the table.

'Hey, careful!' Georgie exclaimed, as a plate slid towards her, nearly toppling over the edge. 'What do you think you're doing, putting your *creation* –'

she paused and flipped her hand dismissively at the blue and silver cakes – 'centre stage? The Years 9s are organizing this, so it's up to us what goes where on the display table.'

'Chill, Georgie. Just because we're running things doesn't mean we have to hog the show,' Ted said.

I could hardly believe it: Ted Watson ticking off his sister for being mean to a couple of Year 8s. Nice one.

'These look great!' he added, smiling at Mads. 'Very original.'

Mads dissolved into the most ridiculous fit of girlie giggles I have ever heard.

I raised my eyebrows and accidentally caught Ted smiling right at me. He rolled his eyes as if to say, 'What is she like?'

'Fine,' snapped Georgie. 'Leave them where they are then.' She turned to me. 'Now why don't you and your little *orange* friend clear off and let us set up without any more distractions?'

I sidled off and made discreet gestures for Mads to follow.

'Georgie was so rude—' I began.

Mads interrupted in a stage whisper. 'Shhh, it's starting!'

107

'Hey, everyone, welcome to the Oakwood High Charity Cake Off,' said Ted, gesturing to the banner behind him on the stage. He laughed nervously.

Everyone cheered. Ted looked at Georgie, who stepped forward.

'Obviously this is for charity,' Georgie said, in a sickly sweet, aren't-we-good voice, 'and thank you all sooooo much for your donations. Today we will be looking to see who's got the X Factor when it comes to baking!' She paused for a reaction, but didn't get one. She looked annoyed, but carried on. 'So . . . It's not just about how your cakes look. A panel of Year 9 judges, including Ted and myself, will taste the cakes and give them scores for style *and* substance!' Again, no reaction to the non-joke. Georgie coughed. 'Anyway, the winner will get a batch of Ted's very own Chocolate-Orange Cake-Pops, and the loser will get Milly Barry's book, *How to Bake* – because they'll need it.' She laughed nastily at this.

'Ted's cake-pops are supposed to be amazing,' Mads hissed.

I raised my eyebrows. 'Seriously? "Ted's cake-pops"?' I repeated. 'Listen to yourself.'

Mads was fixated on what was happening on stage, however, so my sarcasm was lost on her.

The four Year 9s had begun to taste the cakes and were writing things down on clipboards. They had started at one end of the table, so it was an agonizing wait as they nibbled their way through the plates of tempting treats which looked 100 per cent more delicious than ours. I glanced at our (or rather *my*) cupcakes, which I now thought had far too much icing on them, plus the blue and silver colouring was looking a bit sickly. Not that this was the top of my list of worries. The more I looked at our 'creation', as Georgie had called it, the more queasy I felt for another reason altogether: Charlie's 'brilliant plan' for something to replace the peppermint essence was beginning to feel utterly stupid.

He had better not have dropped me in it, I thought grimly.

I held my breath as I watched Ted, Georgie and

their classmates each pick up one of our cakes. They seemed to take an age peeling back the blue and silver paper cases. I crossed my fingers as they took a bite . . . and felt the contents of my stomach rise as I watched the judges' faces contort into expressions of disgust.

Georgie dramatically spat her mouthful out on to the stage behind her.

'Oh! Urgh . . . Oh my goodness!' she spluttered, making a performance of retching as though she was going to be sick. 'What the . . . ? What are these supposed to be?' she gasped.

Mads's hands had flown to cover her mouth. Even beneath the fake tan I could see that her face had gone pale. Her eyes wide with horror, she grabbed my arm and tried to pull me out of the hall. I couldn't move. My feet had grown roots through the parquet flooring.

All around us people were laughing loudly, turning to see who was responsible for making Georgie Watson almost throw up in public.

I wasn't breathing. I couldn't speak. I thought I might actually faint.

'Well, I think we know who the losers are!' Georgie finally announced. She looked straight at me. 'Ellie Haines and Mads Conway for their absolutely gross "Mint-Choc-Chip Butterfly Cupcakes". *Mouthwash* Cupcakes, more like! Do tell us what your secret ingredient is, girls?' she smirked. 'You must have used an unusual quantity of peppermint flavouring in these? As in, enough to *poison the whole school*.'

Everyone roared with laughter and turned to stare at us. I closed my eyes and prayed that when I opened them the nightmare would be over.

When I opened them, however, the nightmare was still very much continuing.

And Mads had gone.

I went straight to my room when I got home. I couldn't face my family. I couldn't face *anything*. Particularly as Mads had vanished without a trace at the end of the day and was now not answering my calls or texts.

I tried to console myself. One good thing had to come out of this disaster: Mads would surely write in to cancel our application for the TV *Cake Off*. Especially if she thought there was a chance that Ted had applied too. There was no *way* she would let herself be humiliated in front of him again.

It wasn't much of a silver lining, though. Mads wouldn't want to *speak* to me after this. I had ruined

her chances at *The Cake Off* and her chances with
Ted in one fell swoop.

I had ruined everything.

I sat up and pulled my sketchbook out from under
my bed. It's like a diary, where I draw and scribble
down things that have happened and stuff about
how I feel. It's a great way to sort out my thoughts:
sometimes I put funny things in it which are
hilarious to look back on, sometimes it just helps me
work things out when I am feeling low.

That afternoon I was definitely feeling low. So
I was sitting cross-legged on my duvet, deep into
drawing a cartoon of the whole school cake-show
fiasco (giving Georgie a huge nose with a massive
spot on the end of it) when Kitkat jumped on to my
lap and curled himself into the space between my
legs. He closed his eyes and set up a deep, rumbling
purr – quite an impressive sound for a kitten that
small.

'Prrrrrr . . .'

'Yeah, you just lie there and look cute. This is

113

all your fault, you know,' I said.

He tucked his tail around him like a black-and-white furry apostrophe. I couldn't help melting at the sight. He was still a baby. What did *he* know? If it was anyone's fault it was mine. I should have checked that the cupboards were shut properly and that the tin's lid was on tight.

I stroked Kitkat's little white head, and his purring went up a notch. He opened his pirate-patch eye. I could have sworn he was smiling at me.

'Maybe having a kitten isn't so bad, little Kitkat,' I said. 'At least you can't get cross with me over boys and baking.'

'ELLLLIEEEEE!'

Our peaceful bonding moment was shattered.

By Charlie.

Who else?

He burst into my room. Kitkat took one look at the fiery ball of energy that was my brother and shot into the air, his fur sticking out all over him, his teeth bared. Then the kitten landed on my thighs and dug his claws deep into my flesh. This was becoming a bit of a habit.

'OOOOOWWWW!' I yelled, leaping off my bed, sending my sketchbook and Kitkat flying.

The kitten let out a similar noise and went harum-scaruming around the room, bounding from chair to desk to bed to bookcase.

'CHAZZER!' I yelled. 'What on earth did you have to come charging in like that for? You've terrified Kitkat.'

Kitkat emphasized exactly how terrified he was by jumping down from the bookcase and immediately peeing on my school bag. Another habit I was growing distinctly tired of.

Charlie dropped to his knees and peered at Kitkat. 'Ah, marking his territory again, I see,' he said.

'Oh for goodness sake, who do you think you are? Crisp Packet? Will you give it a rest? I have had a terrible afternoon and I do not need you in my room. Get out and . . . film some badgers or something,' I snapped.

'It's *Chris* Packet not "Crisp",' Charlie corrected me. 'Anyway, I don't want to film badgers, I want to know how the cake contest went,' he said, pouting.

'Well, *I* don't want to talk about it,' I said.

'Why?' he asked.

Boy, he can be thick sometimes.

'Because it was an epic fail, that's why,' I said. 'If you hadn't told me to put *toothpaste* in the icing, at least they would have been edible. I practically poisoned the judges and now everyone is laughing at me.'

(Yes, that *is* right. I had listened to my stupid little brother and had put dental hygiene products into our cupcakes. So? I did *say* I couldn't cook.)

Charlie shrugged. 'Did you bring any home for me to eat?'

I let out a dry laugh. 'Chazzer, are you even madder than I thought? Didn't you hear me? They were *inedible*. As in, *no one could eat them*. Even *you* could not have eaten them.'

Charlie frowned. 'I don't understand. It was only

116

toothpaste. What's the big deal? Toothpaste tastes of peppermint. You said you needed peppermint flavouring,' he said.

I scowled at him.

'What? It's not poisonous. Is it?' he said. He looked suddenly quite anxious.

'Raow!' said Kitkat.

I turned on the cat. 'You can shut up, too. If you hadn't eaten my first batch of cakes, none of this would have happened.' I looked away. My lips were beginning to tremble and I did not want to cry in front of my annoying little brother. 'I've had it with stupid baking and stupid Cake Offs.'

'You can't give up now!' Charlie said. 'I was looking forward to the party in the garden after the show. I wanted to get Milly Barry's autograph.'

'Chazzer,' I said. 'I. Cannot. Cook. *If*, by some miracle, I got in, I would be thrown out of the place before Sam Parkins could say "What are you waiting for? Bake!" I need to make sure my application is well and truly cancelled. Go and get Mum's iPad. I'll see if there's a number I can call or something.'

Charlie pulled a face. 'I don't think you *can* get out of it now,' he said. 'This is what I came to show you.' He handed me an envelope.

It was a large A4 envelope with a very familiar logo stamped in gold lettering in the top left-hand corner. And it was addressed to me.

I dropped it as though it was a very hot cupcake. 'No,' I whispered.

'What's the matter?' said Charlie. 'I thought you wanted to go on *The Cake Off*?'

'Not after today, I don't!' I cried. 'Haven't you been listening to a word I've said?'

'Well, maybe they're writing to say you haven't got a place,' Charlie said, trying to be reasonable. 'Here, I'll read it for you.'

My brother slid his finger under the envelope flap and tore it open. He drew out a suspiciously thick wad of paper and scanned the top sheet seriously.

He looked up at me, beaming. 'Hey, congratulations! You *have* definitely got a place!

Actually I remember now,' he added. 'They only write to people to say they have been successful. It said so in the small print of the application form.'

He is a total nerd-freak! I fumed silently. Whoever reads the small print? And when did Charlie read the application form anyway?

But then I remembered the message that had flicked up after Mads had sent the application off. Charlie was right.

'Hang on, what does it *actually* say?' I tried to grab the letter from him. 'If I've got a place, then that means Mads has, too, no? We applied as a team. Maybe I can phone them and say she'll go on the show but I can't. I'm sure they can find someone else to take my place.'

Like Ted, I thought grimly.

Charlie shook his head and pointed at the letter. 'This is like a contract or something. It's for you, not you *and* Mads. But then, she would have been sent a separate letter, wouldn't she?' He shook the paper and cleared his throat, then read on importantly.

'Says here that you, Ellie Haines, will be "expected to attend on the date allocated to you unless you have a prior commitment you cannot get out of or a doctor's note and that you have to get your parents to write—"'

'OK, OK,' I interrupted.

I took the paper back from him and peered at the tiny type. 'What is this? There's so much small print and it's so *small* they can't expect anyone to literally read all this, can they? Where's Mads's name?'

'I already told you, this is *your* contract,' Charlie said primly. 'I can't understand why you don't want to do it,' he went on. 'I've been trying to get on TV for years – well, months – and you just enter one thing and get to do it. It's so unfair.'

'Flip!' I said, scanning the letter. I felt as though I had just got off the world's fastest merry-go-round. 'This is a nightmare of the most nightmarish proportions known to humankind,' I said, my voice rising to a squeak.

'Er . . . no it's not,' said Charlie. 'Those floods and

wars and things you see on the news? They're much worse. And Chris Packet says what's happening to our native skylark population is a travesty—'

'LISTEN!' I shouted.

Charlie was startled out of his monologue.

'Mads put me up to this,' I said. 'And Mads's name is nowhere to be seen on this contract. Now, either *The Cake Off* people have made a mistake, or Mads did something stupid and forgot to put her own name on the form . . . or, she has entered me for a joke and didn't enter herself at all . . .' I did not like the feel of where any of these thoughts were going. 'In any case, it was not my idea, so technically I have been entered under false pretences,' I said. I sounded more confident of this than I actually felt. 'I shall have to ring them or email or whatever and explain what's happened and say I can't do it.'

Charlie's expression brightened suddenly. 'I've had an idea. What if I pretended to be you and went on *The Cake Off* instead?'

'It's a great idea, Chaz,' I said with heavy sarcasm.

'Except for the fact that (a) You are a ten-year-old-boy and I am a thirteen-year-old girl AND I THINK THEY COULD SPOT THE DIFFERENCE . . . and (b) You think that toothpaste is an acceptable ingredient in confectionery.'

'I could put on a dress and get a wig and some high-heeled shoes and—'

'Look like a pantomime dame? Great plan! Just shut up and go.'

Charlie pulled a face, but thankfully did as I asked and left the room.

I slammed the door behind him.

At last I was alone again. Well, not entirely alone, of course. Kitkat was still there. He was now mewling because he couldn't find the way back out of my room.

There was a nasty smell coming from my school bag, and another pong from behind the chest of drawers. I only hoped Kitkat hadn't found a mouse and killed it. Surely he was still too small to do that, I reasoned.

I moved the chest of drawers and saw a small dark shape on the floor by the skirting board. I realized too late, as I reached to pick it up, that it was in fact a poo.

Bring it on! I thought, raising my eyes to the ceiling.

I ran to the bathroom to get some loo roll, ran back and dealt with the poo, then ran to the bathroom again to scour my hands with the hottest water I could bear.

Next, I fished out the letter from *The Cake Off* and cast my eyes over it one more time. There was only one thing for it: I was going to have to call Mads and pray that she had received her own separate letter. Then I was going to have to beg her to get me out of this.

I called Mads's home phone as I reckoned someone would pick up, even if it was not Mads. I

123

was right: her mum did. When I asked to speak to Mads I was told, 'She came home in a bit of a state. She's in her room, sulking. Have you two had a fight?'

I swallowed hard. 'No!' I said. Or at least not yet, I thought. 'Can I – *Please* can you get her to come to the phone?' I asked.

'Hmmm, I'll try,' said Mads's mum.

She turned to call for Mads, her hand over the receiver so that her voice sounded muffled. Then, to me, she said, 'She's coming . . . Here, I'll pass you over.'

I heard more muffled chat, then at last Mads came on the line.

'Hey,' she said, dully.

'Hey. I – I'm really, *really* sorry about the cupcakes and Georgie saying they were rubbish and everything,' I blurted out. My words tripped over themselves. 'I should have told you what happened. It was a nightmare – it was all Kitkat's fault. I mean, not the toothpaste in the icing, obviously—'

'TOOTHPASTE?' Mads shouted. 'Did you say "*toothpaste* in the icing"?'

'Er, yeah, bit of a long story . . .'

I filled Mads in on the whole thing, from me coming home to find the kitchen in a mess, to Charlie saying he would help me out.

I finished and waited for Mads to explode on me.

Silence.

There was a tiny squeak from the other end.

'Mads?' I said. 'Are you still there? . . . Please say something.'

'Toothpaste!' Mads squealed.

'I know. It was a mental idea. I'm sorry—'

'Hahahahahahahahaaaaa!' she shrieked. 'Toothpaste in a cake? Your brother cracks me up every time!'

'Mads? Are you joking me?' I could not believe her. One minute she was running out of the school hall, humiliated, not speaking to me; the next she was *laughing* about this?

'Hahahaha! No but, seriously – can't you see

the funny side?' she said. 'Oh my goodness, I can't breathe!'

I felt myself relax. She was not winding me up. Even Mads could not fake that kind of giggling fit.

'Yeaaaah . . . I guess so,' I said. 'I am sorry, though. About the contest and, well, everything. I've got something else to tell you too.'

In for a penny, in for a pound, I thought. I might as well press on, now that I was sure Mads was in a good mood.

'Go on,' Mads said. She was still giggling, but had calmed down a bit.

'I – first of all, have you checked the post today?' I asked.

'No. Why?'

I heaved a sigh of relief. She just hadn't seen her letter yet. 'Right, well, you might want to check now.' I paused, still not sure if I wanted to tell Mads this on the phone. 'Only, I've had a letter from *The Cake Off*—'

'O . . . M . . . G!' Mads squealed. 'We're in? . . .

Mum!' she was shouting now, and it sounded as though she was running. 'WE'RE IN!!'

'Please God, let her have a letter too,' I said to myself. 'What will I do if it's just me?'

Mads was talking to her mum. I strained to catch what they were saying, then Mads was speaking into the phone again. 'No letter today,' she said. My heart plummeted into my Converse. 'But you know what the post's like,' Mads was saying, chirpy as ever. 'It'll probably come tomorrow.'

'Yeah, I 'spect you're right,' I said.

Let's hope so, I thought. Because if that letter doesn't come, my life is officially over.

The next day, Mads was bouncing off the walls with excitement from the moment we met. I had managed to blend in with the crowd at the bus stop before Mads arrived. I had been doing all right at keeping a low profile so far, avoiding anyone who would know about the Toothpaste Icing Fiasco.

Then Mads arrived, running as usual, grinning like a loony, and drawing attention to herself (also as usual). She didn't have the same fears as I did about people spotting her and gossiping. And she was already talking loudly.

'. . . so it *sucks* that I have to wait until after

school. How will I get through the day?' she finished breathlessly.

'Hey, Mads,' I said. I wished she wasn't so hyper. I could hear certain Year 9s whispering and giggling, and I was pretty sure I knew what they were talking about. Mads was oblivious, of course.

'Hey, so have you brought your letter, at least? I need to see it!' Mads said, grabbing my bag.

I tugged it away from her. 'Mads, not here,' I said. I shifted my eyes towards a couple of Georgie's gang who were pushing through to the back of the bus and shooting evils at us. One of them burst out laughing and another shouted, 'Got your breath mints with you today?'

I felt my face go hot and immediately looked away.

Mads either hadn't heard or was ignoring them. 'Come on! You've got to show me,' she was nagging, pulling at my bag as I made my way ahead of her on to the bus.

'Let me sit down,' I urged. I found a seat near the

129

front, as far away from the Year 9s as possible, and slouched low, pressing myself into the corner, up against the window.

Mads was about to slide in next to me when she spotted someone and began waving.

I pulled her arm. 'What are you doing?' I hissed.

Mads sat down with a crash and scowled. 'What has got into you? I was only saying hi to—'

'Hey, you guys.'

I glanced up. Ted. I groaned softly and wished I could vanish into the fabric of the seat.

'Hi, Ted.' Mads swished her hair over her shoulder, which sent it flying across my face and into my eyes. 'Whassup?'

Ted grinned. 'Hi, Ellie – you trying to hide, or something?'

I sat up and flicked Mads's hair off me. 'No,' I muttered.

'Well, you should be,' said a sarky voice.

Georgie leaned over her brother's shoulder and smiled nastily. 'I am surprised you two came in today. If I'd been you, I would have stayed at home and phoned in sick. In fact, I nearly had to phone in sick myself after eating your Mouthwash Muffins.'

'Georgie, can you save us a seat?' Ted said over his shoulder. 'There's not much room back there today.' He squashed himself against Mads's seat to let his sister past.

'Don't worry about her,' Ted said, once Georgie had squeezed past him and flounced to the back of the bus. He gave an embarrassed smile. 'She's pretty excited today.' He leaned in a bit further and whispered, 'She got a letter to say that she's got a place on *The Cake Off* TV show. You know – the one-off charity—'

'Episode for kids,' Mads finished. 'That's so cool! Me and Ellie have entered and—'

'It's brilliant Georgie's got a place!' I cut in. What was Mads doing? Ted would laugh his head off if he knew I had a place after what had happened in the contest at school. I would never live this down.

'Yeah . . .' Ted's smile faltered. 'It is.'

'Oh, you don't seem that pleased?' Mads said. She pouted and touched Ted's arm. 'You entered too, didn't you? Isn't that how you got the idea for the school contest?'

I nearly gasped aloud! So Mads *had* planned the whole thing with an ulterior motive in mind all along. I had been right: this had nothing to do with cheering me up and everything to do with getting herself a boyfriend.

Ted was looking towards the back now, and the bus had pulled away.

'Better sit down,' he said hurriedly. I glanced up at him again. 'Good to see you're OK,' he said, looking at me. 'I thought you might be low after yesterday.' He moved off.

Mads turned to call after him, 'Thanks, Ted! We're cool.' Then as soon as he was out of earshot, she turned on me. 'What did you interrupt me for?' she hissed. 'I wanted to talk to him about me entering *The Cake Off* too!'

'Mads—'

She sank back into her seat and sighed. 'This is just so amazing,' she said, staring at the ceiling. 'Imagine, Ted and me on *The Cake Off* together . . .'

'Don't tell me. You'll be the Dream Team,' I croaked.

'What?' said Mads, snapping out of her romantic imaginings.

'Nothing.'

At least now I had the perfect excuse for getting out of *The Cake Off*. Mads would get her letter and then I would easily persuade her that she did not need me by her side.

Not now that she had Ted to keep her company.

As it turned out, that conversation on the bus was only the first step on the journey towards the End of the World As I Knew It. If I had known how bad things were going to get, I would have actually enjoyed that bus journey and the rest of that day at school. Even though I spent every break-time dodging behind lockers and hiding in the loos

133

to avoid people laughing at me.

Mads wasn't embarrassed at all. In fact she seemed to find everything utterly hilarious. She made such a thing out of laughing whenever anyone made a remark or shouted something at us in the corridors that by the end of the day, people were only directing their remarks at me.

In a way, it was fair enough. After all, Mads hadn't had anything to do with the toothpaste cakes, had she?

I had never been happier to see the end of a school day.

Mads and I walked out together. Despite what had happened on the bus that morning, I told myself to think positive: Mads was my best friend, and she would never hurt my feelings on purpose. She was simply blinded by lurve. (Euw!)

'Boy, am I glad today is over,' I said.

'Me too,' Mads replied. 'I can't wait to get home and check the post!'

'About that . . .' I held her back for a second. 'I'm going to call *The Cake Off* when I get home and say that my application was a mistake. You don't need me anyway.'

'What?' Mads cried. 'But you and I are doing this together. That was the deal.'

I took a deep breath. 'You know that's not true,' I said.

Mads tutted. 'Stop that. We'll be great together. In fact, I had the most brilliant idea this afternoon while Mr Bartlett was warbling on in History – flip, that man is boring.' She giggled. 'This idea is so ace, just call me the Ace of Diamonds!'

I couldn't help smiling. 'Go on, then,' I said.

'So . . . I was thinking, now that Georgie and Ted are in *The Cake Off* too, we could all practise together. It'll be

awesome. We would learn so much from Ted, and I bet Georgie's all right once you get to know her. I wonder how many other contestants there will be on the episode? It's wicked so many people from our school are getting the chance. When me and Ted get our letters too . . .'

She wittered on. 'So many people'? I thought. So far it's only me and Georgie. There was no way anyone else from our school would get a place, surely? That would be too weird.

Mads was still going on and on about Ted: 'Me and Ted' this, 'Me and Ted' that . . .

I cut her short. 'Listen, Mads – I didn't want to say anything because you are my best friend in the entire world, but you have *got* to stop all this stuff about you and Ted. There *is* no "you and Ted" . . .'

Mads turned to face me. I thought for one moment she was going to snap at me; she looked all tight and angry-looking. Then, like the sun coming out from behind a black cloud, she flashed a dazzling smile and said, 'Oh, stop worrying!' Before I could say another word, she had pushed past me and started speaking to someone else.

'Hey! I heard the news – congratulations!'

I wheeled round to see Georgie and Ted walking behind us. And my best mate had joined them, her arm linked through Georgie's, her adoring gaze fixed on Ted.

'So, I was thinking . . . about *The Cake Off* . . .' I heard her say.

All of a sudden I could not face getting the bus.

I turned around and started walking home.

Mads didn't text or call that evening. I was desperate to know if she had got her letter, but every time I called or texted I got no reply. I suspected she was too busy texting Ted and Georgie instead.

I spent the evening in my room, reading and re-reading my letter and contract, trying to find a way of getting out of *The Cake Off*, or at least making sure that Mads got in as well.

Kitkat did his best to distract me, playing with shadows in my room, getting spooked by a spider and jumping skittishly from bed to chair to desk, and back to the desk again.

I was glad of his company – someone I didn't have to talk to, someone who didn't ignore me because of a fit guy in the year above . . .

The more I thought about Mads, and the more time went on with no text from her, the more I convinced myself that she had ditched me completely for Ted and Georgie.

I wound myself up so much in the end that when Mum came back from her run, she found me in my room, the letter crumpled up on my bed beside me, my head in my hands.

'OMG! Whassup, Ellie?' she said. 'You look as though someone's told you you've won the lottery and then phoned back to say it's all a joke!' She sniggered.

I looked up. Mum was dressed in as ridiculous an outfit as ever. She was wearing a yellow-and-orange combination that I hadn't seen before. It clashed even more hideously with her sweaty face than the pink kit had done. Still, I was too upset to care that she looked like a reject from an eighties pop video.

Life had hit rock bottom as far as I was concerned. Even *my* family couldn't make it any worse.

'Ells?' Mum said, her silly grin vanishing. 'It's Kitkat, isn't it? What's he done now? I knew we shouldn't have got you a kitten. It was all Charlie's idea . . .' She tailed off as my face creased up and a tear rolled down one cheek. 'Oh, Ells! She took a step towards me, her face a picture of concern, and put her hand on my shoulder.

That did it. I burst into full-on snotty, gulpy tears.

'Everything's going wrong!' I wailed.

I shoved the letter at her.

Kitkat freaked out at the noise I was making and scarpered. Off to try his luck with Mumbles again, no doubt.

Mum sat down next to me and read the letter. 'Ellie, this is totes amazeballs!' she said, looking at me with a huge smile on her face.

'Mum – don't say that!' I sniffed.

'OK, sorry, it's amazing.'

'*No!* It's not!'

'Of course it is – my daughter on national TV . . . hey, hey, don't cry. What's the matter? Aren't you excited? I know we teased you and everything, but . . . Oh, Ellie! Please stop!'

I was doing that hiccuping crying now: the kind that shakes your whole body and prevents you from being able to speak properly. 'I-i-i-it's a n-n-n-n-nightmaaaaare!' I wailed.

'Miiiaooooow!' Kitkat was back. He still didn't like the noise I was making, though, and had decided to join in, in protest.

'That's enough, you.' Mum grabbed Kitkat and put him out of the room once and for all, then rushed back to hug me. I collapsed into her arms gratefully. Mum gives the best hugs, even when she's sweaty.

I managed to get the crying under control at last while Mum rubbed my back and kissed my head and shushed me.

141

'S-s-sorry,' I said shakily, pulling away. 'I've just h-had a bad couple of d-days . . .'

'Want to talk about it?' Mum said, gently brushing hair from my eyes.

I nodded. 'This *Cake Off* – it was all Mads's idea, and now she's abandoned me for this hot guy in the year above and she's not even answering my texts any more and . . .' I felt the tears well up inside me again.

'OK, OK, slow down,' said Mum. 'Start from the beginning.'

So I did. I told her how fed up I had been lately, and how Mads really seemed to want to fix that; I told her about *The Cake Off* TV show and the school contest and the disastrous cakes. Finally I told her about Ted.

Mum sat and listened and didn't interrupt or make a sound until I had finished. Then she sighed, gave me a squeeze and said, 'Boys do have a habit of getting in the way of friendships, I'm afraid.' She paused thoughtfully and then said, 'But you know, I think you should stick at it with *The Cake Off*—'

'But, Mum! Haven't you listened to a word I just said?'

Mum held up a hand to stop me. 'Listen. Whatever happens, Mads is still your best friend, isn't she?'

'I guess . . .'

'Sometimes people forget about their friends when they're blinded by a crush, but I promise you it won't last forever,' said Mum. 'You and Mads applied together for the TV show, so as far as *The Cake Off* goes, you are still a team. She'll realize that she needs your help if you're going to work together on the show.'

My face crumpled again. 'No, she won't!' I cried. 'I don't think she even *cares* about the show. You don't get it – she's only done this as a way of getting a date with Ted. I can't do this, Mum. You have to get me out of this.'

Mum shook her head. 'No,' she said. 'I think you *should* do this – Mads or no Mads. You will be *so*

proud of yourself when you're actually on the show.
I will be proud of you, too. Mads will realize what
she's been missing soon enough. Perhaps I could
help you practise baking?'

'*You?*' I cried. 'But . . . you can't cook!'

Mum went quiet. I thought I had overstepped
the mark and that I had offended her. She simply
smiled, however, and said, 'No, you're right. Why
don't you talk to Mads tomorrow? Don't text
her again tonight. Wait and talk to her face-to-
face. Explain how worried you are feeling. She'll
understand – you've been friends for too long.
She's not going to let you down.' I tried to cut in,
but Mum ploughed on. 'I guarantee that Ted will
not be interested, anyway. Since when has one
of Mads's crushes ever developed into anything
serious?'

Mum was right about that, at least.

'But why isn't she texting me back?' I asked.

'There could be loads of reasons,' Mum said.
'You know, I'm so glad we didn't have mobile

phones at your age. They do seem to make life very complicated.'

'Mu-um!' I protested. She always blames technology when she doesn't have the answer herself.

'OK! OK!' Mum held up her hands in surrender. 'I won't say another word. Now . . . why don't you come downstairs and watch some telly before having an early night? Things will look much better in the morning, you'll see.'

I did as she said, but I wasn't convinced about the next day being any better.

In the morning I was still upset. I had waited for Mads at the bus stop but she hadn't turned up. Was she sick? Surely she would have texted me if she was? I had ignored Mum's advice the night before and had texted and texted. Then at eight o'clock that morning, I had finally received a weird reply:

Good luck. Ur going to need it.

145

What did *that* mean? Was this because of those stupid cupcakes? Or was this something to do with Ted? I sighed as I jammed some books into my locker.

Then I caught sight of Mads following Georgie in through the school doors like a desperate-to-please puppy. She had even braided her hair to match Georgie's style. I was half boiling with anger and half incredibly sad. I knew she was only doing it to get closer to Ted. I noticed with a stab of pleasure that it didn't look as though Georgie was remotely interested in being friends with Mads. Then I immediately felt bad for thinking that.

I wished I could turn back the clock to the day I had said I wanted to spice up my life. I also wished Ted Watson and his creep of a sister didn't exist.

'Hey, whassup?'

I whirled round. It was Ted; as if he had appeared because I had been thinking about him.

I blushed. 'Nothing. I'm just late . . . I mean,

I can't find my books.' I babbled.

People were filing past me now, pretending to gargle with mouthwash or making gagging noises and laughing. Would they ever forget about those stupid cupcakes? I was going to have to emigrate or something. If I couldn't cope with school and people laughing at me, how on earth was I going to deal with going on the real *Cake Off*? I took a very deep breath to stop myself from giving in to the heat that was rising behind my eyes.

'Ignore them, they're morons,' Ted said. He gave me a reassuring pat on the shoulder, which made me jump. 'At least you gave the contest a go, which is more than most people in your year did.'

I looked at him, baffled. Why was he being kind? Why was he even talking to me?

He grinned. 'I never gave you this, by the way.' He offered me the Milly Barry book.

The losers' prize, I thought grimly.

As if reading my mind, Ted said, 'Listen, I'm sorry about Georgie going on about "losers". She can come

147

off as a bit mean sometimes, but actually this is a really great book.'

"S OK,' I said. 'I knew our cupcakes would be rank.' I tried to laugh to show I didn't care, but it came out sounding weak and shaky.

'I can't believe you put toothpaste in the icing!' Ted chuckled.

My mouth fell open. 'How . . . ?' My voice dried up.

'Um . . . Mads told us,' Ted replied. He looked awkward, as if he had suddenly realized he had put his foot in it.

I couldn't believe Mads had told them! How could she?

Ted tried to smile. 'Hey, it's not a bad idea, though – combining confectionery with dental hygiene – might prevent a few fillings.' He gave an embarrassed laugh. 'Maybe stick to a recipe next time you enter a baking contest, though?' he added, pressing the book into my hands.

I clutched the 'losers' prize' and turned back to

my locker. Could he not tell how awful this was for me? 'I don't reckon there will be a next time,' I said quietly.

'Don't be like that!' said Ted. 'You shouldn't give up on baking so easily. All it takes is practice.'

'Well, according to Mads, *you're* the expert,' I snapped.

What did I say that for? I hadn't meant for it to sound so rude.

Ted looked even more uncomfortable now. 'I like to bake,' he admitted. 'Not the most macho of hobbies, I guess, but it's my thing.'

'Oh, I don't know. Pete Jollyspoon's quite, well . . . he's quite scary, actually.' Look at me, coming out with all the good lines today.

'So, you like watching *The Cake Off*, then?' Ted asked.

Why is he even still talking to me? I thought. He must think I'm mental, now he knows I decorate cakes with toothpaste.

'Er, yeah. I like *watching* it. I just . . .' I trailed off. I couldn't tell him I was going to actually be *on* it.

Ted peered at me strangely. 'Just what? Are you sure you're OK?' he said. 'You look a bit . . . stressed. Is this because of something my sister's said?'

'No.'

'Mads, then? You two are usually glued at the hip, but I have to say she's been spending a lot of time with Georgie recently. Is that it?'

I shrugged.

Ted smiled. 'You're not giving me much to go on here.'

'You'll laugh,' I mumbled.

'I promise I won't. Try me,' he said.

I reached into my locker and pulled out *The Cake Off* letter.

'Please,' I said, as I showed him the letter. 'Please don't tell anyone else. Mads is the only other person who knows, apart from my mum.'

Ted took the letter and read it, his face lighting up as he realized what it was. 'Oh, yeah,' he said. 'Mads told me. Congratulations!'

My face crumpled.

'OK, OK, *not* congratulations,' Ted said hastily. 'Ellie, you are going to have to explain . . . I'm not sure I really get what's going on here?'

So it all came pouring out. The baking disasters, the fact that Mads was ignoring me but I didn't know why . . . I even told him I was worried what Pete Jollyspoon would say to me if I had to go through with the stupid TV show! I could not believe I was telling this stuff to a Year 9, let alone to Ted Watson.

'It's a total nightmare. I can't bake, my best mate who was supposed to help me is ignoring me, and I . . . I don't know what to do,' I finished.

Ted let out a long breath. 'I see. Wow, this makes things awkward. I guess she hasn't told you then?'

'Who? Told me what?' I asked.

Ted chewed his lip. 'Ah . . . It's Mads – she hasn't got a place. Nor have I, as it happens.'

'What?' I couldn't understand what he was saying.

Ted smiled thinly. 'You know me and Georgie

applied together, just like you and Mads did? Well, Georgie got a letter and you got a letter – Mads and I didn't. And if you don't get a letter, you're not in. Remember what it said on the website? They only contact successful applicants? Mads and Georgie even tried calling to find out if there had been a mistake—'

'Mads and Georgie?' I interrupted. 'I don't get it.'

'Yeah.' Ted squirmed, as though he wished he hadn't started telling me anything. 'Mads came round last night when she found out she still hadn't got a letter.'

Mads went round there? And she didn't text me?

'This must be some kind of joke,' I said. 'Why would *The Cake Off* choose me over Mads?'

Ted raised his eyebrows. 'I could say the same about me and Georgie – she can't cook at all! That's why we entered together. Anyway, like I was saying, Georgie and Mads called the production company and they said it's in the small print on the website . . . Only one contestant can be selected per application.'

Flipping small print again! None of this made *any* sense.

Ted suddenly grinned and said, 'I've just had the most awesome idea! Seeing as Mads has promised to help Georgie, why don't I team up with you?'

I shook my head. 'What did you say?'

'I was just thinking: I love baking, you're worried about it – why don't I teach you?'

'I – I thought you said that, but . . .'

Mads had teamed up with *Georgie*? My brain was scrambled.

'Listen,' said Ted patiently. 'I'll teach you a few recipes. It'll be great. I'm free this weekend if that works for you?'

I was still thinking about 'Mads and Georgie' so I answered automatically, without thinking. 'Th-that would be awesome,' I stammered.

Mads and Georgie. Baking. *Together?*

'Great. Saturday? Text me your number and address.'

He scribbled on a strip of paper and handed it to me. It had his phone number on it. I blinked at it.

'See you then.' Ted waved as he walked away.

I waved back.

What the flip had just happened?

The bell rang and I turned towards my classroom. And there was Mads at the other end of the corridor, looking at me as though she had just seen a ghost.

'Mads!' I called. 'Wait for me! I've got to talk to you.'

But Mads just narrowed her eyes, shook her head and walked away.

Mads managed to avoid me all morning. I was desperate to apologize for being chosen for *The Cake Off* without her. I wanted to explain as well that it was Ted who had come to talk to me and not the other way around. The way she had looked at me by the lockers, I was pretty sure she had thought I was trying to make a move on Ted myself.

Everything was spiralling out of control. I had to talk to Mads face-to-face, if I was going to make things right between us.

I was walking past the art room at lunchtime when I spotted Mads at the other end of the corridor on her own. I ran to catch up with her before she saw me first. I didn't want to give her the chance to escape, as she had been doing all morning.

'Hey, Mads, can we please talk?' I panted. 'I'm really sorry about—'

'I hear *you've* got a definite place on *The Cake Off*?' It was Georgie, who seemed to have appeared from nowhere. She gave me one of her oily fake-smiles. 'Looks like we'll be up against each other!' Her voice was deliberately loud, making sure she attracted an audience.

A few of her minions in Year 9 gathered round, and Mads smirked as she saw the colour drain from my face.

'Mads told me she had entered you,' Georgie went on. 'For a *joke!*'

A snigger went around the crowd of hangers-on. 'After all, we all know *you* can't cook.'

'Mads . . .' I took a step towards my best friend, begging her with my eyes to listen. 'Why won't you talk to me? I'm really sorry you haven't got a place—'

'Who told you that?' Mads spat. 'No, let me

guess – that would be Ted, I suppose? I saw you chatting him up this morning.'

'I . . . I . . .'

'I thought Year 9s were – what was it? "Out of our league?" Oh, forget it,' Mads snapped, turning on her heel. 'Enjoy making an idiot of yourself.'

'Mads!' I cried.

'Oh, "Mads! Mads!",' Georgie taunted. 'Why don't you just leave her alone?' she added. 'She doesn't want to have anything to do with you any more. In fact, she's going to help me with my *Cake Off* idea for the Show Piece – aren't you, Mads?'

Mads turned back and sneered, 'That's right. I am. You're on your own, Ellie.'

Noooo! What Ted had said was true!

'Can't wait to see *your* Show Piece,' said Georgie. 'What will it be, I wonder? Dental Floss Delight? Toothbrush Toffee Turn-Over?'

Mads joined in with the laughter as everyone walked away, leaving me standing alone. I could not *believe* she had sided with Georgie Watson over me.

I felt something inside me snap.

Mum is right. I shouldn't give up, I told myself. And if Ted wants to help me win, that's fine with me.

I pulled out my phone and the piece of paper Ted had given me, and fired off a quick text.

If Mads and Georgie wanted a fight, they had got one.

I told Mum what had happened as soon as I got home.

'Oh, Ells,' she said. 'I know it doesn't help to hear this, but Mads will come around eventually. She'll realize how unkind she's being and things will go back to normal. It just might take a little time, that's all.'

'I don't care,' I sulked. 'If Mads wants to spend her time helping that witch Georgie Watson, then let her. I'm going to prove to her – to *everyone* – that I can do this.'

'You go, girl!' said Mum, punching the air. 'That's the attitude.'

I decided to ignore Mum's cringey comment. I was

on a roll. 'I'm going to start by baking something right now,' I said.

'Okaaay . . .' Mum's smile faltered. 'Not cupcakes, this time, eh?'

'No,' I replied. 'I'm going to keep it simple and try a Victoria Sponge.'

Once Mum had left, the house was quiet. Kitkat was snoozing on the sofa and Charlie was out at a friend's.

I opened Milly Barry's book and turned to the recipe for a Victoria Sponge Sandwich.

It promised that 'if you follow this simple, fail-safe recipe, I guarantee you will have a light and fluffy sponge cake that will be the envy of all your friends'.

'You "guarantee" it, do you, Milly?' I muttered, glancing through the list of ingredients. 'Well it seems simple enough. Let's see . . . eggs, flour, caster sugar, butter, cream and raspberry jam.'

I weighed out the ingredients and read on.

' "The easiest approach is the 'all-in-one' method".
What does that mean?' I wondered.

The recipe went on in a rambling way about how
the Victoria Sponge Sandwich is the 'classic cake
that calls to mind fragrant afternoons in the English
countryside, a picnic rug spread out in a sweet
meadow while swallows dip and circle—'

'Blimey, I thought this was a recipe book, not a
slushy romantic novel,' I said to myself. 'Let's skip all
that and get to the instructions.'

The first line said to 'cream together the butter
and the sugar'. I frowned. Cream with butter and
sugar? I thought the cream was for the filling?

I was thoroughly confused.

'So how much cream do I use?' I asked myself. I
scanned the instructions, but it didn't say.

'This is why baking is so difficult,' I muttered
under my breath. 'Nothing is explained properly.
Why tell you to put cream with the butter and sugar,
but then not tell you how much?'

I poured a good dollop of cream into the bowl

with the other ingredients, just to be sure. Then I looked around the kitchen for something to mix it with. Mum had literally no utensils that I knew of, other than the bare minimum. Then I remembered: she *did* have a blender. Mum had gone through a phase of making huge vats of soup in an attempt to get us eating more healthily. It hadn't lasted long, as Charlie had gone on hunger strike, refusing point-blank to swallow even a spoonful of the bog-green offerings Mum had put in front of us. Even Dad had stopped joking around, and told Mum that he would rather drink the bath water after Charlie had been in it than have another bowl of her Spinach Surprise (the 'surprise' being just how disgusting it was, I reckon).

I got down on my hands and knees and sorted through the pots and pans until I found the blender stuck right at the back of the cupboard, stuffed into its cardboard box.

'This'll do,' I said. I felt quite proud at myself for being so inventive.

I unpacked the blender, put the clear plastic top section on to the base and poured the cake ingredients in.

'Better plug it in before switching it on,' I said to myself, feeling prouder by the minute.

I put the plug into the wall and immediately there was a roaring noise and a wet thwack as I got hit in the face by a slimy, buttery mess.

'*Argh!*' The socket switch had been turned on and I hadn't put the lid on the blender. I fumbled blindly for the plug and wrenched it out of the wall. I wiped myself down, scraped the mix out of the blender and managed to get most of it into a tin.

The mixture was watery, with huge lumps floating in it, but as I wasn't sure what it was supposed to look like, I shoved the tin into the oven and hoped for the best.

Just then the phone rang. Hoping it might be Mads, I rushed to answer it.

'Hey, Ells Bells, only me.'

'Oh, hi. Dad, I'm a bit busy—'

162

'Cake for tea, I hear. Mum texted me. Just calling to say I might be a bit late. Not because I'm trying to avoid eating the results of your baking, haha! No, really, there's a horrendous traffic *jam* – fancy some for your cake filling?'

'Da-ad!'

'Sorry, bad *yolk*, I know – haha! Hope your cake is truly *eggshell*-ent—'

Beep! Beep! Beep!

'Sorry, Dad, that's the smoke alarm. Got to go!'

It wasn't really. It was my mobile, but it gave me a good reason to hang up. It was Ted, replying to my text.

Hey Ellie! B with U Sat @ 10 OK?

I texted back, keeping it short and snappy so I wouldn't make an idiot of myself.

Yh cool. Thnx. C U.

I stared at my phone and wondered about texting Mads. I do not know why I even thought about it, really. I knew she wouldn't answer.

My phone beeped, making me jump. It was Ted again.

Wot r u waiting 4? BAKE!

I smiled and began texting back, then remembered I was supposed to be keeping an eye on the time.

'Flip!'

I rushed to the oven and looked through the glass. The sponge had risen and looked pretty good – golden, and as a cake should look.

I turned the heat off and grabbed some oven gloves, then carefully brought the cake out.

How do I know if it's ready? I thought.

I pressed the top as I had seen the bakers do on *The Cake Off* many times. It sagged a bit. Was it supposed to do that? I had no idea. I looked at the time again. The cake had been in for twenty minutes, which is what the recipe had said.

'OK, here goes,' I said aloud.

I could hardly believe I had managed to make a cake without it exploding on me, or without me being driven insane by Charlie or Kitkat.

I got a wire rack from the cupboard and put it on top of the cake as I had seen the bakers do on the telly. I was going to flip the cake over so that it would come out upside down and could cool on the rack.

'One, two, three . . .'

I tipped the cake upside down and . . . SPLAT!

The whole thing fell out in a liquid mush over the gloves, the rack, and all down my front.

I leaped back, yelling 'NOOOO!' as the warm mixture soaked through the fabric of my jeans.

My Victoria Sponge had less of a 'soggy bottom' than a 'molten meltdown'.

'I'm having my own personal meltdown!' I moaned, as I tried in vain to scrape the mixture off me.

Why on earth had I let Mads get me into this mess? Why did I think that listening to Mum was a good idea? Ted had better have some magic spells up his sleeve, I thought, or I might just have to take Charlie up on his offer to pretend to be me and go on the show instead.

The rest of the week at school was just as awful as I had anticipated. I spent most of my time hiding in the loos from Mads and her new BFF, Georgie, and the rest of the time being teased mercilessly by my classmates. The thought of spending time practising my baking seemed like a treat in comparison.

So that was how I found myself up to my elbows in sugar and eggs on Saturday morning, while Ted coached me through what he called 'basic baking'. He had miraculously found an electric whisk at the back of a cupboard and announced we would be making meringues.

'How can you call meringues "basic baking"?' I said. I had to swap hands on the electric whisk. I felt as though my arm would drop off. 'Surely these egg whites are ready by now?'

Ted grinned and shook his head. 'They're still too floppy,' he said.

'What?' I shouted.

Ted leaned across me and switched the whisk off at the wall. 'Lift the beaters out of the mixture,' he said.

'Why?'

'Then you'll see what I mean. You should check the whites every so often anyway. Changes in temperature can affect the way that eggs react, so recipe timings are only ever a rough guide.'

'Oh, great,' I said. 'So now you're saying that even if I follow a recipe to the letter, it won't guarantee that my baking will come out right?'

I lifted the beaters out of the mixture and the

egg whites fell wetly off them into the bowl with a sloppy plop.

Ted laughed. 'See? They're not firm enough to hold their shape as meringues yet. So although the recipe could say "beat for ten minutes", really you need to know what you are looking for. Although in your case,' he added, giving me a playful nudge, 'I'd say it *is* best to follow a recipe to the letter until you start to feel confident about fiddling around with it.'

'I think I learned that one the hard way.'

'Well . . . toothpaste was never going to be the best swap for peppermint essence,' he teased.

'When will everyone forget about the flipping toothpaste!' I cried.

I couldn't help smiling, though. Although I didn't want to admit it, I was actually having a lot of fun. Ted was really easy to get along with. I had never had any friends who were boys before – most of the boys in my year were losers. Ted was different. He was chilled and he wasn't out to impress with rubbish jokes or endless chat about football. He had even claimed to be impressed by the clips of fox cubs playing which Charlie had filmed. And he had shown him a free website where Charlie could set up his own video blog. *And* he loved Kitkat, telling me over and over how lucky I was to have a pet. (He wasn't allowed one because Georgie was allergic to so many things, pets included.) I was beginning to see what Mads might have seen in him . . .

'By the way, have you made it up with Mads?' Ted asked, breaking into my thoughts.

Why did he have to bring that up? I shook my head. 'She won't reply to any of my texts and she blanks me totally at school.'

'I'm sorry,' Ted said.

'Yeah, well. She seems to prefer your sister's company to mine. Anyway, I need to concentrate or I'll have another baking catastrophe,' I said, struggling to keep my voice light.

I didn't trust myself *not* to get upset if Ted kept on talking about Mads.

Luckily there was loads of other stuff to focus on,

and baking with someone who knew what they were doing turned out to be much more of a laugh than I had thought. It had been pretty stressful with Mads making me do everything by hand, and it had been even worse on my own. Still, I was going to have to learn not to get in a flap if I really was going on *The Cake Off*.

I had a sudden image of myself, baking in front of a camera crew with no one to help me. The contest was just a few weeks away. Would I really be ready in time?

'Are you OK?' Ted asked. 'You've gone a bit pale. If it's the egg mix, it will look better in a minute, I promise. Georgie goes weird around egg whites. Says they make her think of snot!'

'Urgh!' I giggled. 'No, it's fine. I was just thinking that I'm enjoying doing this with you, but I'm going to have to do this on my own soon and I don't feel like I'll ever be ready.'

Ted put a calming hand on my shoulder. 'It'll be fine. Now, you'd better get mixing again before all the air goes out of these.'

A few minutes later the mixture was ready to be spooned on to the baking sheet. We had decided to make a Pavlova and serve it up for tea later.

'I can't believe this takes so long to cook,' I said, checking the recipe. 'How come the oven has to be on so low? Surely that's a mistake?'

The book said to cook the meringue for one and half *hours*! Nothing I had baked before had ever taken that long.

Ted looked at the recipe, too. 'No, that's right. 150 degrees C – you could even set it lower and just leave it longer.'

I felt very confused. 'So . . . what should we do?'

Ted blushed. 'Sorry, I'm making things complicated. Let's just follow this recipe. While the meringue is cooking we can whip the cream and chop the fruit.'

It took ages to peel the kiwis and take the leaves off the strawberries. And then we had to cut everything up. Ted was quite particular about how

172

to slice the fruit so that it looked perfect.

'Presentation is just as important as taste,' he told me. 'In fact some people reckon that we taste with our eyes first.'

'What?' I laughed. 'Sounds a bit gross.'

'It just means that if something looks rubbish, it doesn't matter how it tastes – you will have already made up your mind about whether or not you like it just by looking at it.'

So I did as I was told and chopped and sliced as directed. Then we had to whip the cream, which took almost as long as whisking the egg whites.

Finally the Pavlova was cooked, and the cream and fruit were ready. We piled the cream into the gorgeous gooey meringue and carefully decorated it with the fruit.

'Wow,' I said, taking a step back. 'I'm going to take some photos of this. No one will ever believe I helped make it.'

'You *did* make it,' said Ted.

'Only because of you,' I mumbled. I took some

snaps but stopped myself from sending them automatically to Mads: she wouldn't be interested in my baking. She wasn't interested in me at all now that she had Georgie.

'Shall we taste it?' I asked Ted, forcing myself to push aside my miserable thoughts.

'I think we should wait until your mum and dad are here. And Charlie,' said Ted. 'In any case, I reckon we've earned ourselves a break. What do you want to do?'

'Dunno,' I said.

I was knocked sideways, to be honest. I had thought he was only doing me a favour coming round to help because he felt sorry for me. I had assumed he would leave as soon as we had finished baking, but it seemed like he was enjoying hanging out with me as much as I had enjoyed baking with him.

Ted looked at the floor. 'Might sound a bit lame,' he said. 'But what about watching a couple of the old *Cake Offs* to get a feel for the way it works? See what contestants have done in the past?'

I nodded, relieved. Watching TV together would be OK. I wouldn't have to worry about what to say all the time.

Ted beamed. 'Great! Let's get set up then.' He went to the sink to wash his hands. 'We'd better shut the door to stop Kitkat getting in,' he added.

'Good point!' I said. I looked at the beautiful Pavlova, shiny white with fluffy clouds of cream and mounds of glistening fruit. 'I dread to think what would happen if he got his sticky paws on that.'

'It's a good job he's been upstairs in Charlie's room all morning,' Ted said. 'After what you've told me about him getting in the way before, it could have been a disaster.'

Images of cream and meringue splattered around the kitchen made me shudder.

We went into the sitting room and I fiddled around with the controls to find old *Cake Off* episodes on the net.

'Thinking of Kitkat and cake disasters,' said Ted.

'There was one time where a woman tried to make small cakes which went wrong. Not because of a cat, obviously,' he added. 'They were under-baked or something, I think. Anyway, she ended up running out of time and having to improvise. She changed them into cake pops which worked really well. That's where I got my idea for the ones I made for the school contest. That might be a good episode to watch.'

'Fantastic!' I laughed. 'Build up my confidence by showing me other people's disasters, why don't you?'

'Sorry, I didn't mean it like that. Just thought it's good to see how you can turn a disaster into something good.'

'You sound like my brother,' I said. 'He keeps telling me I've got to learn how to make "triumphs out of disasters".'

Ted held out his hand for the remote. 'I'll find the episode if you like. We need to brainstorm some ideas for your Show Piece anyway.'

'At this rate it'll be my disasters which stop me

176

from being on the show at all.' I sighed. 'I'll go and get us some drinks.'

I was really grateful to Ted for taking *The Cake Off* so seriously. It was very kind of him when there was nothing for him in all this, especially when he had wanted a place on it himself – and deserved it so much more than me.

You must think positive, I told myself as I pushed open the kitchen door. Ted has taught you loads of tips and you know you can make your baking look fantastic. If you think positive, nothing can go wrong.

Nothing, that is, unless you have a kitten who is magnetically attracted to food.

'Oh. My. Word,' I breathed.

I stood in the doorway, my mouth gaping in disbelief. On the table, where once there had been a magnificent meringue with the most mouth-watering decorations, was now what can only be described as a catastrophe: 'cat' being the operative part of that particular word . . .

177

'KITKAT! HOW COULD YOU?' I cried.

The kitten had been bottom up in the Pavlova when I walked in the room. He was not just up to his ears in cream, but up to his neck, tummy and back paws too.

At the sound of my voice, he did a backwards somersault of panic. He leaped into the air and landed – *splat!* – back in the middle of the creamy chaos where he appeared to be stuck, as though swallowed up by a white volcano, only his head now visible.

His face was no longer black and white: his pirate patch was completely covered with the white dessert. The only parts of his body which were distinguishable from the pudding were his terrified, blinking blue eyes and his little pink tongue, which flickered nervously around his lips.

'*No!* Where on earth was he hiding?' Ted came running at the sound of my wails of distress.

'I have no idea,' I said miserably. 'I am so sorry, Ted. I thought he was still curled up on that beanbag

 178

in Charlie's room. I should have checked he wasn't hiding in here before I shut the door.'

Ted shook his head. 'It's not your fault. Wow, I can see what you mean about him now. Not such a cute little guy, at *all*.'

Kitkat was now mewling as he wriggled to get himself out of the sticky mound that had once been our perfect Pavlova.

I sprang into action and grabbed him before he could free himself and make a merry mess all over the kitchen. 'You are a *nightmare*,' I said, as I held him high in the air.

Ted put out a hand. 'Ellie, don't be hard on him. He's only a kitten. He doesn't understand.'

'I know, but I am *sick* of this! It's hard enough learning to bake, but one way or another this cat has sabotaged nearly every single thing I have done.'

I was about to dump Kitkat in the washing-up bowl when the doorbell rang.

'Not now! Who could that be?' I cried.

'I'LL GET IT!' Charlie's voice rang out from

179

upstairs. There was a hammering of footsteps as he charged to the front door.

'I can't believe this animal,' I muttered, holding Kitkat out at arm's length.

Ted squeezed my shoulder. 'Give him to me,' he said. 'I'll clean him up. You deal with the Pavlova. We'll just have to start over.'

I nodded silently and turned away while Ted rinsed a struggling Kitkat and bundled him into a tea towel.

I could feel tears welling up. A small sob escaped my lips. This was the last straw. I balled my fists into my eyes: I couldn't bear to lose control in front of Ted.

Ted put Kitkat down gently and turned towards me. 'Come on, it's not that bad. No use crying over a crushed cake!' He gave me a hug.

There was a snigger from the kitchen door.

'Get you and your cosy date!'

Ted dropped his arms and we jumped apart.

'Georgie,' said Ted. 'What are you doing here?'

180

'We're going to the cinema, remember? Mum said you were here.'

Ted blushed. 'Yeah, course. I was just coming. We're almost done.'

'Looks like it,' said another voice.

I felt my heart leap into my throat. 'Mads?'

My oldest friend had been hovering behind Georgie with Charlie. She stepped forward, hands on her hips. 'Good to see you've been having fun.'

I swallowed. 'This isn't what it looks like . . .'

'They've been cooking together,' Charlie piped up, 'because you won't help Ellie any more.'

'Chazzer,' I snarled. 'Go away and take Kitkat with you.'

Charlie, for once, seemed to realize something serious was going on, and did as he was told.

'What a *sweet* couple you make,' said Georgie. 'Doesn't look like Ted's "lessons" have paid off, though,' she added, with an emphasis on the word 'lessons' as though she thought something quite different had been going on.

'Hey!' said Ted. 'That's enough.'

Georgie waved a hand at him to shut him up and went on. 'I mean, if that's the results of your efforts, you've hardly improved since those rank Mouthwash Muffins you entered for the school Cake Off, have you, Ellie?'

'It was Kitkat,' I said quietly.

Ted took a step towards his sister. 'Just stop it. We've had a disaster here.' He motioned to the squashed Pavlova. 'I said I would help because Ellie's really stressed at the moment and it's not long before she has to go on *The Cake Off*.' He frowned at Mads. 'And it *is* true that you abandoned her, Mads.'

I don't know whether it was Ted sticking up for me, or him mentioning *The Cake Off*. Probably both. In any case, I couldn't stop myself: I could feel sobs working their way up from deep inside me now. It was no good: I couldn't stop the tears. I wished the kitchen floor would open up and swallow me whole.

Ted put a protective arm around me. 'Don't,' he whispered.

'Oh, give me a break, Mr Knight-in-Shining-Armour,' said Georgie. 'Are you coming or not? We're going to miss the film.'

She made to grab Ted's arm, but he pulled it back. 'I've changed my mind,' he said. 'I don't want to go. You're being a nasty—'

'Whatever,' Georgie cut in. 'Come on, Mads. You can have Ted's ticket.'

I gulped back a sob. If Mads went with her, that would mean she had one hundred per cent chosen between me and Georgie. *Forever.*

Mads was glaring at me as though I was the mess, not the Pavlova. Then she turned her back on me and said, 'Yeah, I think I will take that ticket, thanks.'

Georgie gave me a particularly nasty smile, and the two of them left, slamming the front door behind them.

I was too stunned to speak.

Ted let out an embarrassed cough. 'I'll – er – I'll start the clearing up.'

'N-n-no way,' I stuttered through my tears.
'Charlie can do it. It's his fault the flipping kitten was
in here in the first place. I told him to keep Kitkat in
his room, no matter what. You were there, you heard
me. I wouldn't be surprised if he let Kitkat in here on
purpose. No one is on my side, Ted! *No one!*'

I grabbed a kitchen chair, scraping it noisily across
the tiled floor and sat down heavily.

'I am on your side,' Ted said quietly. 'And I know
that *you* know Charlie isn't to blame. You're just
upset.'

'I-I-I know,' I hiccuped, drying my eyes with my
sleeve.

'In any case, it just so happens that your naughty
kitten has given me the most excellent idea for a
Show Piece,' Ted went on, a smile spreading across
his face. 'Unless you already had a plan for that?'

'What do *you* think?' I asked.

Ted raised his eyebrows. 'OK, how about we clean
up first? I wouldn't want to let the *cat out of the bag*
right away . . .'

184

I sniffed. 'What?'

Ted nodded at the squashed meringue and then looked at me, while miming a cat washing its paws.

'You mean . . . ?' The penny finally dropped. 'Ted, you are a genius,' I breathed. I brushed my tears away.

Ted shrugged. 'With my baking skills and your ace artistic gifts, together we can turn this *cat*-astrophe into a truly spect-*cat*-ular Show Piece,' he said.

'Have you met my dad?' I asked. 'Because your jokes are *almost* as bad as his.'

'I'll take that as some kind of weird compliment,' said Ted.

I thought of my kitten struggling to get out of the mountain of cream and meringue and chuckled.

It was an image that was too good to waste, that was for sure. 🐈

I looked up at the multicoloured bunting that I knew so well from the TV programme. I felt I needed to pinch myself hard.

In so many ways it was a miracle I was there, not least because of Dad's obsessive car-parking habits. I swear he treats it like an Olympic sport. If there was a medal for Getting Your Car As Close To the Venue As Possible, he would win gold every time. Even though it would take him all morning to achieve it.

'Matt, I have to say you have done us proud,' said Mum. 'Couldn't have got us any closer unless you had driven us right into Pete Jollyspoon's arms. Not that I would have complained if you had,' she added, giggling.

'Mu-um!' I groaned.

Ted laughed. He leaned in and whispered, 'Your mum's cool. But don't tell her I said that.'

'Don't worry, I won't,' I muttered.

Ted had insisted on coming, and I was glad, however mortifying Mum and Dad were being. If I had only my family with me, I would probably have refused to get out of the car. Ted was doing a good job of keeping me (kind of) calm and was a great distraction from Charlie. My little brother was so overexcited, if Ted had not been there I might have actually killed him.

'We do get to go to the party in the garden at the end of the show, don't we?' Charlie wittered. 'I can't wait to get everyone's autographs. Do you think they'll let me film it? I could put it on my website.'

Charlie had been obsessed with 'developing' his video blog website ever since Ted first introduced him to the idea a few weeks ago. It had been a great idea because it had meant Charlie concentrated on filming Kitkat's antics instead of filming me baking. The weird thing was, he had had loads of hits on his website already. Who would have thought that one naughty little kitten could turn out to be such an internet sensation? I had to admit to being a tiny bit proud of my brother. Not to mention intensely grateful to Ted.

I was *so* not going to let Charlie ruin the day with his filming obsession, though.

'Chazzer,' I said warningly. 'If you even *think* about getting your camera out during the party, I will force Mum and Dad to take you straight home.'

Deep down, I wasn't sure I would survive until the party anyway. My nerves had churned me up so much I felt as though I might keel over at any moment.

Dad stepped in. 'Charlie, let's go and look at those famous squirrels you always see on the TV programme. Perhaps you can film them instead? Coming, Kate?'

'In a minute,' said Mum. She was hovering near the entrance to the famous Tepee. 'I want to see if Pete will come out and say hello to everyone.'

The mere thought of meeting Pete Jollyspoon in real life made my stomach churn even more. I backed away from the tent . . . and into Ted, who grabbed my hand and squeezed it reassuringly.

Dad looked at Mum, and then gestured pointedly to me and Ted. 'Kate,' he said. 'I think we should go. Now.'

Mum looked annoyed but said, 'OK, OK, I'm coming.'

As I watched my family walk away from the Tepee, I wished they could take me with them.

I turned to Ted. 'I think I should leave.'

'Don't start,' Ted teased. 'It's going to be awesome!' He made his way into the Tepee with the bags he had been carrying, forcing me to follow. 'I bet no one else has your artistic skills,' he added. 'I *know* Georgie doesn't.' He looked sad as he said this.

'Hey, what's up?' I asked. I took the bags from him

and plonked them on the work surface.

'Georgie was a nightmare again this morning,' he said. 'She told me I was a useless brother and said I had "no sense of family loyalty". She's right, of course,' he added.

'Oh, flip! I'm sorry,' I said. 'This is all my fault—'

'No, she's the one being an idiot,' Ted said. 'Anyway, it's not as though she hasn't had help – Mads is a great cook. It's just – I'm kind of dreading her being here too.'

'Hmm.' I didn't trust myself to say any more than that. *He* was dreading Georgie being there? How did he think *I* felt? The past few weeks had been so stressful. Even though it seemed like everyone at school had finally forgotten about the Toothpaste Incident, I still missed Mads like crazy. We had never had a falling out like this before. I looked around anxiously, wondering when Georgie would arrive.

Ted nudged me. 'Hey, did you hear what I said?'

'What?'

He rolled his eyes. 'You're on another planet! I

asked if you needed a hand sorting out this lot,' he said, gesturing to the bags.

'I – I dunno . . . I feel a bit sick actually,' I said. 'Why don't you do *The Cake Off* instead of me? You were the one who was supposed to get a place on the show. I reckon Mads was too. It's all just a terrible mistake. I think I might go and talk to someone and explain.' I made a move, but Ted stopped me, grabbing my wrist.

'Ellie,' he said. 'You've had loads of practice. You'll be fine. You'll be more than fine, you'll be—'

Ted had stopped abruptly. 'It's Sam and Sid!' he breathed.

I turned slowly, my heart pounding, to see the famous television presenters heading straight for us, looking exactly as they did on camera. Sam was wearing his trademark ripped jeans and white T-shirt, his black-rimmed glasses framing his mischievous, sparkly eyes. Sid was wearing a red-and-white stripy top and jeans and was grinning through his floppy blond fringe. They were both coming towards us.

'Hey, guys!' called Sam. 'Welcome to "the Tepee"...' He hooked his fingers around the words. 'So, you must be Ellie Haines?' he added, 'Unless this tall, handsome bloke is a girl in disguise?'

'No, it's me,' I said, raising a hand as though I was in class. Why was I being so lame?

'I hope you've not smuggled in an extra pair of hands,' Sid joked.

'Sorry?'

'Your friend here,' said Sam, nodding at Ted.

'No, no, I'm just . . . er, carrying Ellie's stuff,' Ted mumbled. 'Could I – Would it be OK if I had your autographs?'

Sam beamed. 'Of course you can.'

'And then you must leave. Or –' Sid paused and raised one eyebrow – 'we shall have to kill you,' he said, in a fake Russian-spy voice.

192

'Yeah, sorry, of course,' Ted blustered. 'Didn't mean to get in the way.'

'He's *joking*!' said Sam. 'It's only Pete "Mister Laser Eyes" Jollyspoon who does the slaying around here . . . Joke again!' he said hastily, as Ted looked even more worried. 'Have you got a pen and something to write on?'

'Oh, right.' Ted coughed to hide his embarrassment. 'Hang on a minute.' He dug around in his pocket. 'Here,' he said. 'Could you write it "To Ted and Ellie"?' he asked.

I looked at him sharply, but he refused to meet my eyes. 'Ted and Ellie'? A fluttering started up in my chest like a whole field of butterflies.

I looked away and tried to distract myself, and immediately saw something guaranteed to make my heart beat faster for quite a different reason.

Georgie had arrived. With Mads in tow.

Mads's expression when she saw me was definitely of the 'if looks could kill' variety. She did not look that happy with Georgie either, however.

Georgie had made a big entrance to draw attention to herself, and was now loudly telling Mads what to do with her bags.

She left Mads slaving away, and sashayed over towards me. While Ted was still talking to Sam and Sid, she took the opportunity to hiss, 'Well . . . look who it isn't? Ellie "the Pain" Haines. I didn't think you'd have the guts to turn up today after your latest baking disaster.' She tittered. 'I hope you've checked your stuff to make sure your dirty little kitten hasn't snuck his way in today. Actually,' she added, 'I hope you *have* brought him with you. It would be *hilarious* to see him make a mess of your cooking on camera!'

Ted had finished talking to Sam and Sid, and now turned to his twin, looking awkward. 'Hey, Georgie,' he said. 'Good luck for the competition.'

Georgie snorted. 'Like you mean it.' She looked me up and down. 'We all know you want your little *girlfriend* here to win, so spare me the Mister-Nice-Guy act. Mum and Dad are outside. Why don't you

194

go and see them? Unless you've turned your back on *all* the family?'

Ted's face had gone white. 'I – Georgie . . . There's no need to be such a—'

'Such a what?' said Georgie, squaring up to him.

Thankfully Sam came over to say hi. 'Do you two know each other?' he said.

Georgie took a step back and immediately her expression was one of 'butter wouldn't melt'.

'Oh hi, Sam!' she cooed. 'It's soooo good to be here. Thank you *soooo* much for giving me this opportunity. It's like a dream come true! It's been such a journey to get here—'

'Oh, right?' Sam cut in. 'So where do you live?'

Georgie's crocodile smile faltered. 'I – no, I meant it's been, like, such an *emotional* journey, you know?'

'Ah, an *emotional* journey,' Sam said. 'OK.' He winked at me. 'Well, good luck, girls! I'll leave you to get settled.'

Ted was doing his best to bite back a smile as Georgie, visibly deflated, said, 'Yeah. Sure.' She went to join Mads, who was busy lining up an impressive array of coloured icing and a sheaf of paper. I guessed that was Georgie's crib sheets containing the recipe for her Show Piece.

Mads looked really miserable: Georgie seemed to be laying into her. I couldn't hear what she was saying, but whatever it was, Mads clearly wasn't happy.

The sooner Mads and Ted left, the better. I just wanted to get the show over and done with. Once we were baking, I wouldn't have time to worry about Georgie – or anyone else, for that matter.

Thankfully, Sam was already steering my former best friend out of the Tepee, all the while chatting away with her so that she didn't realize she was being kicked out until she was actually at the exit.

Ted took the hint and whispered, 'Better be off, too. You'll be great, Ellie. I'll have everything crossed for you!' He crossed his eyes, his legs, stuck his tongue out, and tried to cross all his fingers too.

I laughed. 'Thanks, Ted.'

Georgie mimicked me from the other side of the Tepee. ' "Thanks, Ted." '

Ted frowned, touched me lightly on the arm and added, 'See you when it's all over for a celebration.' Then he kissed me quickly on the cheek and ran out of the Tepee before I could react.

Sam caught my eye and winked again. 'You've got a great boyfriend. Very supportive!'

'He's not my boyfriend,' I said, blushing.

I could feel Georgie's eyes burning through me.

'If you say so,' said Sam, arching one eyebrow. 'So, you two,' he went on, talking to both me and Georgie now. 'Even though your friends have left, you're not alone. Sid and I will be around the whole time the show is being filmed, so if there's anything you need, we're here for you.'

Sid was welcoming another baker into the Tepee now – a boy – and was politely asking his supporters to hurry up and leave, while Sam stayed to chat and help me unpack.

All the work stations were decked out in different

197

colours. Mine was red, Georgie's was blue, and the other contestant had yellow. The kit on the stations matched the work surfaces, so my mixer and bowls and utensils were red too. Red was my favourite colour, so surely that was a good sign, I told myself.

'Where are Milly Barry and Pete Jollyspoon?' I asked Sam, as I emptied the last of my stuff on to the work surface.

'Oh, probably still in make-up. Takes ages to cover up all their wrinkles,' said Sam, deadpan.

I didn't know what to say to that.

'Don't worry, we love each other really. All that banter you see on the TV is even worse off camera, I can assure you. But it doesn't mean a thing. We're worse than school kids in the playground.'

I laughed uneasily.

At that moment a woman in black trousers and T-shirt came bustling over. 'Five minutes till camera,' she told Sam, and started fiddling with the lapel on his jacket.

'Steady!' Sam said, making a show of backing

198

away from the woman. 'Don't touch what you can't afford.'

The woman ignored him, concentrating instead on fixing a mike on my top. She rushed off, talking into her headset. All the people racing around me were not helping my nerves to settle.

I must have looked every bit as anxious as I was feeling, because Sam put his head on one side and said, 'Sid and I get the jitters before filming too, you know. Once the cameras start to roll, you kind of forget about them. Honest! There are too many other things to think about. Like having fun. And you *will* have fun, I promise. Especially when you find out who our star judge is.' He grinned mischievously and made a move to talk to the others.

'Star judge? What do you mean?' I called out to Sam. I didn't know if I could take any surprises. 'Where are Milly and Pete? Are they not judging today?'

'Oh yes. They'll be here in a minute. Pete's probably out shooting the squirrels.'

199

I gasped.

'Not really! Blimey, you are gullible. We did use to have a huge problem with sugar-addicted squirrels, though. Not any more. It's all squirrel-proof and guarded by an anti-rodent squad, like a version of the CIA except for squirrels. It's nuts!'

I gave a shaky laugh.

'Right, enough nattering,' said Sam. 'Time to crack on! Are you ready?'

'As ready as I'll ever be,' I said.

Which is never, I thought, grimly.

S am and Sid were taken off by a technician to do
the pre-recorded links. Sam had explained that
the show would have to be edited down before it
went on air.

'You'll be baking for hours,' he had told me. 'The
programme would be far too long if we put the
whole thing out uncut!'

'Does that mean you'll only show the best bits?' I
had asked.

'And maybe the worst,' Sid had joked.

At least, I hoped he had been joking.

I could hear them now outside the Tepee saying
things like: 'One hour left to go, bakers. One hour

left!' and 'OK, bakers, fifteen minutes left. That's one-five minutes left.'

'Makes you feel sick, hearing them say that, doesn't it?'

It was Georgie, taking her chance to come and unnerve me, just as I had thought she would.

I took a quick look at the other contestant. He was peering closely at a piece of paper, frowning in concentration. Probably having a last-minute read-through of his recipes – as *I* should be doing, I thought.

'He's Ravi, by the way,' said Georgie. 'You see, *I* have actually bothered to talk to him, rather than spending my time sucking up to Sam like *you*,' she sneered. 'It's not going to make any difference creeping up to him, you know. He's not judging your baking.'

Oh yeah, like you weren't totally schmoozing him yourself earlier, I thought. But I didn't dare say it aloud.

'I know he isn't,' I muttered. I looked at the clock

that hung from the centre of the Tepee. When would we be able to start? Once we were cooking, Georgie would have to leave me alone.

'I suppose you and my idiotic brother have practised enough – in between all the smooching?' she went on with a smirk. 'Don't think I haven't told Mads what's been going on. She's furious, you know. I doubt she'll ever speak to you again now that you've stolen Ted from under her nose. Mads has been filming me, by the way – to get me used to the cameras,' she added. She gave a toss of her long mane of hair as if the cameras were trained on her there and then.

I racked my brains for something clever to say in return, but thankfully Sam and Sid came in before I could say anything I would later regret.

'OK, bakers!' said Sam raising his voice above the scurrying people and chatter going on around us. 'We will begin filming for real in half an hour. That's thirty minutes, bakers.' He flashed both hands three times to make the point.

'Hello, everyone!'

All the chatter stopped immediately: Milly Barry had arrived.

'My word, you do look nervy, all of you,' said Milly. 'Don't be – it's supposed to be fun.'

Milly Barry was exactly the kind, grandmotherly figure I had always imagined her to be – though she was a lot trendier and smilier than any gran I had ever met in real life. Her hair was white-blonde and perfectly blow-dried, and her lips were shiny, with a raspberry-coloured lip gloss. She even had a chic French manicure too.

'We'll just have a little chat before the cameras roll,' Milly was saying, 'so we can put you at your ease before the competition begins. Pete's just coming,' she added.

'Still having his hair done, is he?' quipped Sid.

'Stop it, you!' said Milly. 'Let's introduce ourselves while we wait,' she went on. 'What's your name, dear?' she asked me. 'Tell us a bit about yourself and what you're going to do today. We'll ask it all over again on camera, so think of this as a little dress rehearsal.' She smiled warmly and nodded at me.

Pete Jollyspoon chose that moment to walk in. He looked as stern as he always did on the TV.

'I – I'm Ellie Haines,' I stammered. 'I'm thirteen. I never was much of a baker and then my –' I paused, avoiding Georgie's gaze – 'my friend entered me for this contest. I love baking now, but I'm worried that I'm not good enough to be here. I'm going to be doing macarons and my Show Piece cake which I'll – I'll keep secret for now.' I stopped, worried I had said too much.

Everyone laughed, but in a nice way, and clapped. Only Georgie gave a snort of disgust.

'Well done, Ellie,' said Milly. 'Nice to keep an element of surprise.'

'I hope you are going to do something original with your Show Piece,' said Pete. 'The macarons are a bit simple for *The Cake Off*.'

I felt the blood drain from my face.

Milly tutted. 'Take no notice, Ellie dear. Now, you two . . .' She turned to Georgie and Ravi. 'Tell us a bit about yourselves too.'

'Baking's not about personalities,' Pete grumbled.

Milly ignored him. 'Now then, what about you, dear?' she asked Georgie.

Georgie swished her hair and gushed that she had been baking 'ever since I could hold a wooden spoon'.

Liar, I thought.

Ravi said he had watched his parents and grandparents cook all his life and had 'drawn inspiration' from them.

Sam sidled up to me. 'You're looking a bit peaky, kiddo,' he whispered. 'Not thinking of throwing in the tea towel over a couple of comments from Pete, are you?'

I shrugged.

Georgie and Ravi seemed so cool and collected. I thought I must be the only person in the room feeling so wobbly I might as well have entered myself in the competition as a Show Piece Jelly.

'OK, everyone ready?' said a technician. 'Cameras stand by . . .'

I watched as immediately Milly, Pete, Sid and Sam seemed to switch on their Television Faces: they were so alert they looked as though they were about to run a race and were waiting for a starter gun to fire.

'. . . and three . . . two . . . one, you're on!'

'Hello! Welcome to this special SportsFundUK edition of *The Great Junior Cake Off*!' said Sam. 'Today we are in the South-West of England. Three lovely young bakers have been selected from hundreds of applicants across the region and we're sure they're going to knock our socks off with their baking skills, so get phoning and donate as much money as you can for this excellent good cause!'

'That's right,' said Sid. 'And today's special episode is going to be even more exciting than usual, as we have a surprise star guest coming to help with the judging after the Show Piece round!' he added.

'Woooooo!' shouted Sam. 'So it sounds like these talented kids have everything to bake for, Sid?'

'They certainly do,' Sid agreed. 'I reckon we shouldn't waste any more of their valuable time. Are you ready, bakers? Are you steady, bakers? . . . Then, what are you waiting for . . .?'

He paused then shouted, 'BAAAKE!'

We had to do three different recipes. The first round was 'Individual Party Cakes'. Ted and I had practised macarons for this as Ted reckoned Milly and Pete would be impressed by a traditional French recipe. 'They are sophisticated,' he had told me. 'And *The Cake Off* loves sophisticated.'

I had made them so many times by now that I felt I could probably do them in my sleep. For the show I had gone for a pistachio recipe, as the colour was so amazing – a bright pea green. Ted had taught me how to make a scrumptious ganache filling flavoured with more pistachios. They came out pretty well, though I say so myself.

I wished Ted was there to reassure me. I couldn't even text him as we had been asked to hand in our phones to security when we arrived so that we couldn't cheat.

Pete and Milly had us bring our creations up to the table in the middle of the Tepee. I watched as Ravi and Georgie went ahead of me. They looked so pleased with themselves. I prayed that I wouldn't trip over on my way to the table and send my macarons flying.

'What a talented bunch you are,' said Milly. She smiled encouragingly as I set my plate down.

'We haven't tasted anything yet,' said Pete.

Milly took no notice of him and picked up a slice of Ravi's raspberry and almond traybake. 'These look delicious,' she said. 'Raspberry and almond is always a favourite with me.' She took a bite and made appreciative noises. 'Lovely,' she said. 'Very moist, and you've got the combination of flavours just right.'

That's it, I thought. Ravi is going to win this . . .

 210

But Pete was pulling a face as he chewed. 'Hmmm, a bit *too* moist for my liking. I would say this is a little underbaked.' He picked up another slice and turned it over, giving it a good prod. 'See how my finger sinks in here?' he said.

Poor Ravi's face had fallen. He nodded.

'Pete doesn't like a soggy bottom,' Sid said to camera.

Pete glowered. 'Our star judge won't be impressed if this is the best you can do,' he said. 'The edges of your traybake are cooked, but the middle slices are not.'

Ravi picked up his plate and went slowly back to his work station.

'Never mind, dear,' said Milly. 'I loved it.'

Sam patted him on the shoulder as he walked past.

Pete turned to Georgie. 'Let's see if you've done any better with your cupcakes. Talk us through them, please.'

Georgie beamed. 'These are an invention of mine,'

she said with pride. 'I call them Volcano Cakes.'

Invention of Mads's, more like, I thought. They sounded like the kind of over-the-top crazy idea Mads would have.

Pete was looking doubtful. 'I hope they're not going to erupt in my mouth,' he said. 'So, how does this work?' He picked up a small jug of sauce which Georgie had placed next to her cupcakes. 'The cakes have a hole in the middle, so I'm guessing that is where the sauce goes?' he asked.

Georgie nodded. 'Yes. Just pour it in, stand back and see what happens.' She stuck her chin in the air defiantly.

Pete's expression hardened. 'We aren't in a chemistry lab, young lady.'

'Chill, Pete!' said Sid. 'Cooking *is* chemistry.'

'Yes, look at the chemistry between you and Milly,' added Sam, in a nudge-nudge-wink-wink voice. Milly laughed.

I wished I could laugh too, but all I could think of was that I hoped the cakes would be an epic fail. I know that was mean, but they looked so impressive next to my boring old macarons.

Milly took a dramatic step back as Pete poured the contents of the jug slowly into the hole in the centre of one cupcake.

Nothing happened.

Georgie's proud smile wavered.

'Good job this isn't your Show Piece,' said Pete. 'It's hardly what I would call impress— Oh!'

The cake erupted violently and the red sauce burst out in an arc, splattering the front of Pete's blue shirt.

Milly hid her mouth with her hand, but I had already caught her giggling. Sam and Sid bit their lips and tried not to smirk. Sam handed him a cloth.

Pete grimaced. 'Well, I hope they *taste* good,' he said, brushing at his shirt with the cloth. He picked up the cake, which did look like a very realistic mini volcano by now with red lava-like sauce trickling down its sides.

I held my breath as Pete bit into it.

He reacted much the way Georgie had done to the Toothpaste Muffins: immediately spitting out his mouthful into his hands.

Reeling back from the table, coughing and spluttering, he said, 'They are DISGUSTING! What did you put in them?'

Georgie looked as though she wanted to run. For a moment, I actually felt sorry for her.

Sam leaped to her defence, putting a protective arm around her. 'Come on Pete, don't be so mean. The girl said they were explosive cakes – they've done what it said on the tin.'

'You have to give her credit for style and originality,' Milly added. 'Although –' she looked apologetic – 'I don't think I'll be tasting one.'

'I don't blame you. They taste like acid!' Pete cried. He wiped furiously at his mouth as if to erase the taste.

Georgie was bright red. 'I think that might be the vinegar,' she said in a low voice. 'You mix it with baking soda to get the explosion. I thought the

214

raspberry juice would make it taste sweet—'

'VINEGAR? In a CAKE?' Pete exclaimed.

Sam hurriedly pushed my plate of macarons towards him. 'Let's see what Ellie has done,' he said.

Georgie slunk behind Sid as though wishing she could become invisible.

Now it was my turn before the firing squad. What if I had a nightmare, too? Pete was too busy fussing with his shirt to bother even looking at my creations, though.

Milly was looking encouraging. 'Cheer up,' she said. 'It's the cakes we are eating, not you.' She picked up the smoothest macaron and inspected it. 'The shape is perfect and you have not overfilled it, either,' she said. 'Pistachio is a favourite of mine.' She took a bite. 'Delicious!' she cried, once she had finished her mouthful. 'So sweet and light. These would look just wonderful on the table at a party. Very sophisticated.'

I could not help smiling. Ted would love that comment!

'So, bakers,' said Sam, stepping forward to hide Georgie who was having a bit of a meltdown now. 'Let's get ready for the next round while Pete cleans himself up.' He made a show of backing away from Pete as if he was a dangerous wild animal, but winked at us as he did so.

The next round was more straightforward, as we all had to bake a Victoria Sandwich. I had certainly had enough practice with this. After I had spectacularly failed on my first attempt at home, I had told Ted what I had done and he had roared with laughter.

'You put cream in *with* the eggs and sugar?' he said. 'What on earth made you think of that?'

'The recipe said "cream together the eggs and sugar",' I explained.

Ted shook his head. 'You numpty. That is a cookery phrase which means that you beat the eggs and sugar together until they make a creamy mixture.'

It was at that point that Ted had realized I really did know nothing about baking, so following the Pavlova disaster, he had gone right back to basics and explained everything very, very clearly.

I now knew that the key to the perfect 'Vicky Sponge', as Ted called it, was to weigh the eggs in their shells and then weigh out equal quantities of flour, sugar and butter. This was a fail-safe method which even 'numpties' like me could make work every time.

Luckily for me, Milly Barry was impressed with this method. 'I must say, that is a very old-fashioned way of baking. I can say that because it's the one I always use,' she confided.

Poor Ravi had a second round of 'soggy bottom' complaints from Pete, and Georgie's cake was pronounced 'over-baked'. Milly, however, complained that Pete was being far too hard on them.

'At least they taste good,' Pete admitted grudgingly.

The comments on my cake were better than the rest, although Pete could not resist saying it had a 'slightly dense crumb'.

I should have felt more confident by the end of this round, but Georgie was shooting me such evils, and we still hadn't met the mysterious 'star judge' yet, either. Who could it be? I still had to bake the Show Piece, and I couldn't stop my hands from shaking. I hoped the secret guest would be kind like Milly and not another tough guy like Pete.

'The next and final round is the one we've all been waiting for,' Sid announced. 'But before we start, I think we all need a bit of a rest. Bakers – let's have a cuppa and put our feet up. Follow me!'

We trooped out of the Tepee and into a smaller marquee, which was just as colourful and jolly. A table was laid with cups and saucers, plates and cake forks and a couple of large, steaming teapots.

'This is my favourite bit,' cooed Sam, licking his lips as he scanned the table which had been laid with our cakes from the first two rounds. 'Tuck in, everyone!'

I couldn't eat a thing. I watched as the camera crew and sound technicians dived into the display. They made appreciative noises, devouring what we had made (although everyone avoided the Volcano

Cakes, I noticed). I looked at Georgie, who was trying her best to seem as though she didn't care, but it didn't help that Pete was still muttering about the explosion to one of the crew.

'If I had wanted a demonstration on how to make molten lava, I would have gone to the Science Museum,' I heard him mutter.

I decided I should do the right thing and try to cheer Georgie up. She might have made my life hell over the past few weeks, but we were in this together now. I walked over to where she was standing.

'Don't know about you,' I said, 'but if I don't see another cake ever again, it will be too soon.'

'That's OK for you to say,' she spat. 'Milly loved your macarons *and* your sponge.' She narrowed her eyes. 'But there's still the Show Piece round to go. And I intend to win. This is my big chance to prove to Mum and Dad that it isn't only my precious twin brother who can be brilliant. I am not letting anything – or *anyone* – get in my way.' Then she turned on her heel and walked out of the marquee.

220

'Hey! Where are you going?' I called out.

'To give myself a break,' she said over her shoulder.

As I watched her leave, I suddenly realized I knew exactly how she felt. I was doing this partly because *my* brother always got the attention in the family, too.

If anyone had asked me even a day ago if I wanted to win this competition, I would have laughed and said that I only wanted to get through it without making a fool of myself.

But now that I had spent so many hours practising and practising to get everything right, I knew it mattered to me more than anything to win. I felt exactly as Georgie did: it was time for me to get some attention for once.

We went back into the Tepee, all of us very subdued now. Sam and Pete were doing their best to cheer us up with silly comments about Pete's 'silver fox' hair and how he and Milly should be married.

None of us reacted to the banter: we were all far too focused on the task ahead.

'OK, bakers? All refreshed and ready for the final round?' asked Sid.

We nodded and muttered, 'Yes . . .'

'Sound a bit more enthusiastic, can't you?' crowed Sam.

'YES!' we shouted.

'Well, what are you waiting for . . . BAKE!' Sid yelled.

And we were off!

I started laying out all the ingredients I needed for my Show Piece.

Black roll-out royal icing – check.

White icing – check.

Ingredients for the cake itself – check.

I then looked for my crib sheets to turn to the instructions that Ted and I had written down.

Everything I needed to know was on those sheets of paper: how to make the cakes, how to cut them to make my design, how to decorate them, the timings for each stage.

They weren't there.

I scrabbled furiously through the remaining things in the bag and ended up turning the contents out on to the floor. I riffled through the items, my hands shaking, panic taking over my whole body. Where *were* the sheets of paper? I had had them for the two previous recipes. This was a disaster! I needed my drawings for the design, my time sheet, the recipe for the cakes I needed to make, and now I couldn't find them anywhere!

I gestured to Sam to come over, telling myself to stay calm and that I would quietly ask him if anyone had been near my stuff.

There was a niggling doubt in the back of my mind: what if someone had tried to sabotage my Show Piece on purpose? Surely not. No one would think to look for those sheets of paper, would they?

Maybe a member of the crew had tidied them away while we were having tea?

The minute I saw Sam coming towards me, I thought of Georgie leaving the tea tent. What had she said? That she needed to 'give herself a break'. I had thought she'd meant that she needed some air. What if she had meant something different? That she needed to give herself a *lucky* break – by stealing my crib sheet?

I groaned and put my head in my hands. What could I do? I couldn't accuse her of stealing on camera. What if I was wrong? I would look like an idiot. A lying, mean-spirited idiot.

I closed my eyes and tried hard to remember the instructions Ted and I had written together, putting all my energy into recalling his advice and the things he had said when we were baking together.

'What's up, kiddo?' asked Sam. 'You've got everything to play for now, you know—'

'I can't do this,' I blurted out.

Sam immediately put his back firmly towards the

camera, which was panning round, filming all of us. 'Is this one of those moments where I have to throw a jumper over you or start swearing to make sure this bit doesn't make it to the final cut?' he said quietly. 'Because if it is, don't worry. We've been there before – disasters happen on this show all the time. You won't be the first.'

'I bet I'm the first to have lost their recipe notes,' I said. I swallowed hard. There was no way I was going to be one of those losers who cried on telly.

Sam beamed. 'Oh, is *that* all? Don't worry about that. My infamous hypnotherapy techniques will bring back your memory, no problem.' His face became suddenly very serious and he waved a hand in front of my face, saying, 'Look into my eyes, look deep into my eyes . . . in a moment you will fall asleep and when you wake up, you will remember your recipe . . .'

'What are you up to now, Sam?' It was Sid who had come to see what was going on.

'Shh! Can't you see I'm hypnotizing Ellie, here?' said Sam.

'No you're not. You're being an A-grade loony,' said Sid.

'Even hypnotism can't help me now,' I said. I took a deep shuddery breath. 'I've lost my crib sheet for my Show Piece.'

Sid put an arm around me and said, 'You know what you need to do? You need to GET A GRIP, my friend!' He laughed for the benefit of the camera. 'Seriously, though. I'm sure you've practised this a million times, haven't you?'

I nodded, not trusting myself to speak.

'OK,' said Sid, sounding business-like. 'So talk me through it. What do you have to do first?'

'I – I have to make two sponges,' I mumbled.

'Good,' said Sam. 'We know you can make a super-duper sponge, so you get cracking with that. Ha! Get *cracking* – with the eggs! See what I did there?'

I smiled in spite of myself. 'You are just like my dad,' I said.

'Oh dear,' said Sam with a dramatic grimace. 'Dad humour is seriously bad.'

 226

'This is not the time for rotten yolks!' said Sid.

We groaned.

He had lined up the ingredients I needed for a Victoria Sponge. I thanked him and got going with weighing the eggs as I had before. Then I measured out the flour, butter and sugar.

'There you go,' said Sid. 'You just needed to get started. Now it's all flooding back, isn't it?'

'It's rather like when we forget our lines for the start of the show,' said Sam. 'Sometimes all it takes is for someone to prompt us with one or two words, and then we find we remember everything in a rush.'

I smiled gratefully. 'Thanks, I think I'll be OK now.'

Really I was still feeling daunted by the task that lay ahead. What if I couldn't remember how to cut up the cakes to make the shape I needed? What if the whole thing looked a mess and didn't work? Ted would be embarrassed to admit he had ever helped me. Georgie would revel in my failure forever. Charlie would never let me forget it: now that he had his website up and running, he already thought he was the bee's knees. If I failed on TV, I would never live it down.

I made myself think about the design I wanted to end up with.

'Can I have some more paper?' I asked, once the sponges were in the oven.

Sam went and fetched some for me and I found the pen Ted had put in one of the bags.

'Boy, you are relaxed,' Sam teased, watching me scribble away. 'Look at this, Sid!' he called out. 'This girl is so chilled she's doing a spot of doodling while she waits for her cake to cook!'

I caught Georgie from the corner of my eye – she

was giving me a particularly sly smile.

'I – I'm tweaking my pattern for my cake, that's all,' I said.

'Show your sketches to the camera!' Sid urged. 'Let's see what you're planning.'

'No,' I said, covering the page with my hand. 'I told you – I want to keep it as a surprise.'

Georgie flashed me a look as if to say, 'Yeah, right – you have no chance.'

That did it. I *knew* she had taken my crib sheet. I went hot with anger at the thought of her doing this to me, especially after I had tried so hard to be nice. I felt a surge of determination as I told myself I could do this. I could make a Show Piece to end all Show Pieces. I could win. All I had to do was concentrate.

I felt calmer once I had an image on the page. Drawing always does this to me: I almost go into a trance when I get into the flow. I was focused now. I was on a roll. Nothing could stop me.

Ping! The timer went off and the sponges were ready. I got them out to cool and started rolling out the black-and-white icing, checking my sketch every so often to remind myself what I was aiming for.

Once the cakes were cool, I cut a circle out of the middle of the larger round cake. Next, I carved the smaller cake into the shape I needed. I mixed up some butter icing to use as a kind of glue and spread it thinly over the carved cakes. Then I transferred the rolled-out white fondant icing on to the cakes, smoothing it with my hands.

Finally I cut out the right size of black, pink and blue fondant icing shapes and then with a toothpick I drew in the final details. I used a small clean paintbrush with a bit of water to make the fondant gummy where I needed to stick one colour of icing on to another. For the last few details I used a regular paintbrush dipped into a food-colouring mix to paint on some decorations.

'When you paint on top of fondant icing,' Ted had told me, 'you need to add lemon juice to your food colouring instead of water. This won't disintegrate

230

the fondant and the lemon juice just evaporates away, so you get a brighter colour.'

How he had picked up all this information I do not know, but every single one of his tips had worked out so far.

'Five minutes left!' Sam suddenly called out. 'Five minutes!'

My heart started pounding again.

Five minutes to make sure my cake was perfect and securely placed on the presentation plate.

I was racing against the clock now. I realized with a jolt that I hadn't even taken a look at the others' cakes. I had been concentrating so hard; I had been in a world of my own.

'Five . . . four . . . three . . . two . . . one – step away from the cakes, please. Step away, Georgie! That's it,' Sam demanded.

I quickly threw a clean tea towel over my cake to keep it a secret until I had to reveal it to the judges. I stole a quick look at what the other two had done.

Georgie curled her lip at me and stepped back

with a dramatic gesture towards her cake. 'Ta-daaah!' she announced.

I gasped. There was no way I could compete with what she had created. I glanced quickly at Ravi's. He smiled shyly, but his cake looked amazing as well.

I prayed and prayed that I had remembered the recipe properly, if only to get back at Georgie.

'Now for the moment we have all been waiting for!' said Sam. He bounced up and down on his toes. 'I'm so excited, I can't tell you,' he cooed. 'We have had to keep this a secret for so long, but finally—'

'You know what?' said Sid, butting in, much to Sam's obvious annoyance. 'Seeing as this is a special *Cake Off*, for charity and all that, why don't we get the contestants' families and friends into the Tepee to share this magic moment?'

'What a lovely idea,' said Milly.

Pete did not look as though he agreed, but Sid jumped in quickly and said, 'Great! I'll go and get them, and Sam can bring in our mystery star guest once everyone is here.'

This was prolonging the agony as far as I was concerned. Why could they not get on with the judging and let us all go home?

I held my breath as Mum, Dad, Charlie, Ted, Mads, and Georgie and Ted's parents shuffled into the Tepee with Ravi's family close behind.

They were all grinning and looking about as uncomfortable as if they were about to be asked to bake a Show Piece themselves.

'OK, huddle up, huddle up,' said Sid. 'Imaginary drum-roll please! Let's hear it for our wonderful star judge ... IT'S ... *LARRY FILES*, FROM THE WORLD-FAMOUS BAND, WRONG DIRECTION!' He whooped and clapped like crazy, while Mads screamed and Georgie looked as though all her Christmases had come at once. Ted's eyes were wide with surprise and Charlie was struggling with his camera case, while Mum fought to make him keep still.

Larry sauntered into the Tepee and flashed a very white-toothed smile from under his trademark floppy fringe. 'Hi, guys.'

'Hey, Larry!' said Sid. 'Welcome to this episode of the SportsFundUK Charity *Cake Off* – and thanks so much for taking time out from your busy schedule to judge the Show Pieces. I'm sure I speak for all of us when I say how excited we are that you're here.'

I caught Mads's eye and she grinned at me and held her hands to her chest and mouthed: *I am in love!* I rolled my eyes, but felt a warm glow at seeing Mads looking so happy for a change.

Maybe things would be OK after all this was over.

'Can we get on with the judging now?' Pete asked grumpily.

'Absolutely, man,' said Larry. 'I can't wait to dive into some cake.' He rubbed his stomach and grinned.

'Let's look at Ravi's first,' said Milly. It really does look incredible.'

Ravi's cake was made to look like the planet Saturn with the rings and everything! He had covered it in a swirly mix of different-coloured icing, and when Pete cut into it, the inside of the cake was multicoloured too.

I am well and truly finished, I thought as I took in Milly's beaming face, and Larry's appreciative expression. Even Pete looked a little impressed. (He had stopped frowning, anyway.)

'What an ambitious project!' said Milly, as she cut through the sphere. 'I love the way the cake is striped inside. Very clever.'

Ravi was looking pleased with himself – until Pete bit into the cake and pulled a face. 'What is this flavoured with?' he asked.

Ravi's smiled faltered. 'I – I thought orange would be a good flavour as I've put chocolate icing through the middle. Orange and chocolate go well together—'

Pete snorted. 'I would suggest you use orange juice and zest next time, instead of a *synthetic* flavouring. This is too overpowering.'

Milly looked at Ravi sympathetically. 'It is a stunning cake, though, Pete,' she said.

'I am not interested in Style Over Substance, Milly. You know that,' Pete retorted.

I bit my lip as I thought of Charlie saying the same thing to me, and tried hard not to look at my little brother, who was grinning from ear to sticky-out ear.

Larry took a chunk of Ravi's cake and chewed thoughtfully. 'Yeah, it is kind of a bit too orangey,' he said. 'Sorry, man.'

Ravi nodded sadly and the judges moved on to Georgie next.

Georgie's cake was unbelievable. I had no idea how Mads could have come up with such an amazing design. It was a Barbie Princess cake: a real Barbie doll was standing up in a cake that had been shaped to look like a princess's gown, and Georgie had decorated it with glitter and hearts and flowers.

I closed my eyes for a second and fought to keep the tears back. This was it, I knew it. Georgie was going to win. Mads would be able to say that she and Georgie were the Dream Team, and I would have lost my best mate forever.

I heard a gasp from everyone in the Tepee and snapped my eyes open.

Milly had been about to cut into Georgie's cake – the knife was still poised mid-air – when the plastic doll lurched to one side. The decorations were sliding off the fondant icing so it looked as though Barbie was about to lose her skirt too. The next thing I knew, Barbie had fallen to one side with a sticky *flop*, causing the whole cake to collapse. Georgie let out a howl of anguish as Larry Files said with a snigger, 'Looks like Barbie's been partying a bit too hard!'

'Yes,' Pete agreed. 'She looks wiped out.'

Georgie sobbed, while Sid and Sam put their arms around her.

Milly frowned at Pete and Larry. 'Let's see what it tastes like. The proof of the pudding is in the eating, after all.' She cut into what remained of the skirt. 'Ah,' she said, as the rest of the structure collapsed. 'It is, erm, a little bit underbaked.' She pointed to the raw, squishy cake inside. 'Next time you do need to think about making sure that the structure of the cake is firm enough to cope with holding up the doll, dear,' she said gently.

'This is *your* fault!' Georgie growled, turning on Mads. 'But then, you never really wanted me to win, did you? I should have known. This was all a plot to make sure that your pathetic little BFF over there would win instead, wasn't it?' She pointed at me.

Mads's face was as white as the roll-on icing on Barbie's skirt. 'I never – I don't know what you mean!' she protested.

Everyone in the Tepee started talking at once.

'I don't think that's very nice of you . . .' Mum piped up.

'Wow, a fight on *The Cake Off*!' cried Charlie. 'I need to get this on film . . .'

'Hey, guys, chill,' said Larry. He stepped in between Mads and Georgie and slung his arm around Mads's shoulders. She went from white to bright red. 'I think you had better leave this poor chick alone,' Larry said, glaring at Georgie.

'But she—'

'OK, OK, that's enough!' Pete said, raising his voice above the commotion. 'Everyone be quiet, please.'

Georgie tossed her hair. 'This whole thing is a set-up!' she shouted. Then she turned and stormed out of the Tepee, her parents, clearly upset too, running behind her.

Ted watched them go and then fixed his eyes to the ground. I couldn't get him to look at me. What was he thinking?

Pete waited for the hubbub to calm down. 'We haven't seen the last cake yet,' he went on. 'Ellie has been waiting very patiently. Let's take a look at her Show Piece.'

'Too right, Pete,' said Sam. 'The show must go on.'

'Okaaay . . .' I unveiled the cake, drawing back the tea towel very carefully, praying that everything had stayed together.

There was a whoop from Sam and a round of applause from Sid.

'Awesome!' said Larry.

Then everyone joined in the clapping and cheering. I blushed.

'Intriguing!' said Milly. 'A tiered cake, iced and painted to look like a basket . . . with something struggling to get out, I think. May I?' she pointed at the basket lid.

I nodded.

She gently lifted the lid and everyone gasped.

'How cute is that!' cried Larry. 'A kitten in a basket – and all made of cake.'

'What on earth made you think of doing that?' asked Milly.

'Well, my own kitten . . . he's kind of food-obsessed,' I said shyly.

'He is!' said Charlie. 'You should take a look at the films on my website—'

'Charlie,' said Dad. 'Not now.'

I smiled at Dad gratefully and carried on. 'When I was practising before coming on *The Cake Off*, my cat got into a Pavlova I had made and—'

240

'Sorry?' said Sam. 'You'll have to run that past me again – your cat GOT INTO a Pavlova?'

'Er, yes,' I said. I was really embarrassed now. I wished the judges would hurry up and taste the thing. Pete's expression was not encouraging; if anything he looked reluctant to taste the cake at all.

'If the cake tastes as spectacular as it looks,' said Milly, 'I think we are in for a treat.'

'Let's hope it doesn't taste as *cat*-astrophic as it looks,' said Pete.

'I don't know,' said Larry. 'I'm *feline* quite tempted.' He chuckled while everyone groaned.

'*Purrrrrr*-leese, leave the jokes to us, guys!' said Sid.

Milly tutted. 'Let's get back to the matter in hand, shall we?' she said.

She brought the knife down right through the centre of the cake and pulled out a huge slice so that she and Pete could inspect the 'crumb' and the 'bake'. Pete peered at it, poked it and prodded it and finally pronounced, 'So far, so good.'

241

The three judges each broke off a piece and took a bite.

'Mmmm!' Milly licked her lips appreciatively. 'So light! So fluffy! And what a delicious vanilla flavour to the butter icing.'

Pete was nodding. 'Not bad,' he said.

'Now that is high praise indeed!' said Sid.

'Lush,' said Larry. 'You can come and bake for me any time!'

Mads was jumping up and down, giving me the thumbs-up.

'I think we know who the Top Baker is, don't we?' said Pete.

Milly nodded. 'I think so. But we'll need to confer first. Larry, come with us.'

The three judges went out of the Tepee while a buzz of excited conversation started up among the families and friends on the sidelines.

The judges seemed to take forever.

I was sure that Pete had not been convinced by my Show Piece. I probably shouldn't have told

242

everyone that it had been inspired by Kitkat jumping into a real cake. Then again, I was pretty sure Milly had meant it when she said it was 'spectacular'.

As the minutes ticked away, I was beginning to think Ravi would get Top Baker after all. Pete had been a bit rude about the flavouring in his planet cake, but Ravi had used so many more technical tricks than I had. I had simply made a couple of sponges and then iced them cleverly. What if he thought I had committed that sin above all sins: Style Over Substance?

Finally Milly, Pete and Larry came back in and beckoned to Sid and Sam to join them. There was a quick whispered exchange.

Sid turned to face the camera. 'OK, Larry is going to do the honours.'

Larry stepped forward. 'Thanks for having me on the show, guys,' he said. 'It has been wicked. So, the judges have conferred, and . . . I am really happy to be able to announce that . . .' He grinned and said to the camera, 'This is like *X Factor* all over again!'

Everyone laughed.

Larry went on. 'The Top Baker of *The Great Junior Cake Off* for the South-West region, is . . .' He paused again.

I closed my eyes and prayed that he would get on with it and that I would not cry, whether I won or lost. If I lost, that was tough, but at least I had made it on to the show and I had done my best. No one could say that I hadn't tried . . .

'. . . Ellie Haines!'

I opened my eyes. 'What?' I cried.

'Yes, you, madam!' said Sam. 'Come on, group snuggle!' Then he and Sid enveloped me in a massive bear hug. 'The cameras have stopped rolling now,' Sam whispered in my ear. 'It's all over – well done!'

'Well done, dear,' said Milly, coming over to shake my hand. 'I thought it was inspired of you to take something which had been a disaster in your practice and turn it into such a success.'

'I told you!' Charlie shouted.

Larry put one arm around me and placed the

coveted *Cake Off* giant silver egg whisk in my hand. 'You're a star,' he said. 'Can I have your autograph?'

I giggled. 'Only if you sign one of yours for my best mate over there,' I said, nodding to Mads.

Larry grinned at Mads. 'I think I can manage that,' he said. 'I've got another prize for you, as it happens. Something you can share with your friend.' He fished in his pocket and brought out some pieces of paper. 'Two tickets to our next gig,' he said. 'And backstage passes so you can meet the rest of the band.'

Mads squealed and clapped her hands.

Pete came to shake my hand as well. 'You can really bake, young lady,' he said. Then he actually smiled!

Mads rushed to hug me while everyone else crowded around my Show Piece. 'I *knew* you could do it. And I'm sorry I let you down,' she whispered in my ear.

'It's OK.' I said. 'Really. Do you think . . . I mean . . . could we be mates again?'

'*Best* mates,' Mads said, squeezing me tight. 'I've missed you so much, Ellie. I've been such an idiot!' She pulled away from me and looked into my eyes. I thought she might be about to cry.

'Don't you start!' I laughed. 'You'll set me off.' I hugged her again. A huge weight had been lifted from my shoulders. 'Go and get that autograph then,' I said. I gave her a push towards Larry, who was talking to Mum and Dad. 'And please don't let Dad tell Larry any awful jokes!'

'I'll make sure he doesn't,' Mads said, grinning. Then she bounced over to her idol, barely able to contain her excitement. It was so good to see her happy again and to know we were still friends.

'Well done, Ellie.' Ted had been hovering just behind Mads. I blushed: I had not thought to thank him yet.

'I couldn't have done this without you, Ted,' I started. 'You're the Top Baker really. I should have told everyone how much you helped me.'

'No, *you're* the one who did it. And no thanks to

246

my sister, or so I hear. Sam just told me about the instructions going missing, and I found these under Georgie's work station.' He held out my crumpled crib sheets. 'I'm so sorry, Ellie. I hope we can still be friends?'

I bit my lip, then before I could think about it, I leaned forward and gave Ted a kiss on the cheek.

'I'll take that as a yes then,' he said with a sheepish grin.

I looked over to check if Mads had seen. She was too busy giggling and flirting with Larry, thank goodness. My heart skipped a beat as I wondered if she would have second thoughts about us being mates again if she had seen me kiss Ted.

Dad was gesturing to me to come over and join them.

'Charlie's got one more surprise for you, Ellie,' said Dad. He nodded to my brother who ran out of the Tepee and reappeared moments later with a wicker basket.

'This is why Dad wanted to park so close,' said

247

Charlie. 'Luckily he slept all the way here, so you had no idea he was in the car with us.'

'Miaow!' came a sorrowful sound, then a little black and white face peeped out of the top.

'You haven't . . . you *have*!' I cried. I picked Kitkat up from the basket and cradled him in my arms.

'EVERYONE!' Charlie shouted. 'You have to meet the real star of *The Cake Off* – Kitkat!'

'We thought he should come and share in the glory, seeing as he was so inspirational,' said Dad.

'Is someone going to explain why there is a live cat in the Tepee?' asked Pete.

'It's obvious, isn't it?' said Sam, stroking Kitkat's head. 'This little fella is the icing on the cake!'

'Thanks for bringing him, Charlie,' I said, as everyone cooed over my naughty little kitten. 'In fact, I never thought I would say this, but thanks for making sure I got a kitten for my birthday, too. If it wasn't for Kitkat, I'm sure Ted wouldn't have come up with the idea for the Show Piece.'

'That's OK,' said Charlie. He took Kitkat from me

248

and set him on one of the work surfaces. 'It's cool that he got on TV, too isn't it? Even if it was only the cake version!'

I sighed and shook my head. 'You and your TV obsession. By the way, I hope you're not too jealous that I got to go on TV. It's always been *your* ambition, after all.'

Charlie screwed his nose up. 'Nah. I don't care,' he said. 'I had over one thousand hits on my website last night,' he added. 'Who needs TV when you have the worldwide web?'

I ruffled his hair. 'You're all right sometimes, little bro,' I said.

'Everything good, Ells?' said Mads, coming over with Larry. Sid and Sam joined us, too.

'What do you think?' I said, laughing. 'I said "I just wish something *exciting* would happen to me," didn't I? I guess I got what I wished for! Thanks to my crazy brother and my mad-as-a-hatter best mate.'

'And your boyfriend,' said Mads, nudging Ted and winking.

249

I blushed. Ted grinned and put his arm around me.

'Actually, I think the prize should really go to Kitkat,' I said, trying to change the subject.

'You can't say fairer than that!' agreed Sid. 'In fact from now on, I declare this episode shall be known as "The Great Kitten Cake Off".'

'Brilliant!' agreed Sam.

'Hey, where is that cheeky kitten anyway?' asked Larry.

'He was right here a moment ago,' replied Charlie, spinning round to look for Kitkat.

'Miaooow!'

'Where *is* that coming from?' asked Mads.

'Oh no!' I cried. Kitkat's pirate-patch face was peeking out of my Show Piece basket. He was licking the ear of his fondant-icing kitten twin and was purring happily. 'Kitkat!' I wailed. 'Not again!'